Suddenly Kane lifted his head, breaking the kiss with a hoarse curse.

His eyes were darker now. Not like the sky anymore, Margo thought, but like the sea—a dangerous place, where a woman could drown.

"I shouldn't have let that happen," he said, holding her at arm's length, as though he didn't want her touching him again.

Margo fought not to flinch at the pain that realization brought her. "No harm done."

He slid his palm to her neck, stroking her with fingers strong enough to squeeze the life from her body. Skilled enough to make her body come alive in ways she hadn't imagined possible.

"Damn it, Margo," he muttered, "you didn't even ask if I killed those people, all those years ago...."

Her stomach lurched. "Did you?"

His eyes went bleak. "I honestly don't know...."

Dear Reader,

This month a favorite author from the Silhouette Romance line, Charlotte Moore, makes her Shadows debut—and what a debut it is!

In *Trust Me*, heroine Margo Stafford is afraid to trust the man who tells her to do just that. For Kane Rainer is somehow linked to her eerie new home and the dark secrets it harbors. But how? Is he destined to fight the forces at work to destroy her? Or is he in league with them? She doesn't know, aware only that when she is in his arms, the answers cease to matter.

Enjoy this thrilling, chilling novel—and come back next month to take another walk on the dark side of love…only in Silhouette Shadows.

Yours,

Leslie Wainger
Senior Editor and Editorial Coordinator

Please address questions and book requests to:
Silhouette Reader Service
U.S.: 3010 Walden Ave., P.O. Box 1325, Buffalo, NY 14269
Canadian: P.O. Box 609, Fort Erie, Ont. L2A 5X3

CHARLOTTE MOORE

Trust Me

Published by Silhouette Books
America's Publisher of Contemporary Romance

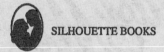 SILHOUETTE BOOKS

ISBN 0-373-27062-3

TRUST ME

Copyright © 1996 by Charlotte Lobb

Books by Charlotte Moore

Silhouette Shadows

Trust Me #62

Silhouette Romance

Not the Marrying Kind #975
Belated Bride #1088
The Maverick Takes a Wife #1129

CHARLOTTE MOORE

has always enjoyed putting words on paper. Until recently most of these words have been nonfiction, including a weekly newspaper column, which has recruited nearly twenty thousand volunteers in the past twenty years for some four hundred different local nonprofit organizations.

When she is not urging people to get involved in their community, Charlotte divides her time among writing, volunteering for her favorite organizations (including Orange County Chapter of Romance Writers of America), trying *not* to mother two married daughters and sharing her life in Southern California with her own special hero, Chuck.

Dedicated to
Kathryn, Jane and Bette,
with thanks for all the love and laughter
we have shared

CHAPTER ONE

Heat waves rose from the sidewalk into the midnight darkness. Along the street a row of eucalyptus trees released their pungent scent, an imperceptible breeze skinning one dry leaf against another in a dusty sigh. Reflected city lights gave the sky an eerie orange glow as heavy tropical air pressed down on Torrance, a suburb south of Los Angeles, shortening tempers and straining nerves.

Dry lightning flashed in the distance.

In spite of the heat, Margo Stafford shivered. Even as a kid in Iowa she'd been afraid of thunder and lightning. After thirty-some years, she still couldn't entirely put away her fears.

She hesitated in front of the two-story building. Her body tensed and her hands turned clammy. Who would have thought the city fathers, in their wisdom, would have selected an abandoned mortuary to be a shelter for the homeless? Refurbishing the old hotel around the corner would have been a far better choice. But no, the senior-citizen lobby had landed that plum for themselves as part of the downtown redevelopment project. Now Margo was charged with turning this derelict building into something livable for women and children who had nowhere else to go.

And the place gave her the creeps.

Particularly since as on-site manager she had to live there. Starting tonight.

She shuddered at the thought. No way had she intended to arrive here so late, but the fund-raising event in Ventura for a sister shelter had lasted much longer than she had anticipated. Then the traffic on the freeway had been brought to a standstill by a horrendous combination of accidents and construction.

Somehow she'd simply have to deal with this bad case of the jitters.

It was only wild tales being told around town, Margo told herself. Just dark jokes. Ghost stories. Witches' covens. Mysterious goings-on. All of the whispers pure fiction. A mortuary provided a ready-made target for every sick comic around.

Except every time she'd been inside this building, her skin had crawled and the hair at her nape had risen to shivery attention. She didn't like the Miller Mortuary. Not one bit. But it was her job to make the shelter a success. She needed an income; she needed a roof over her head. This job provided both. For herself and for others.

She went up the steps to the front door. Juggling her suit jacket over her arm, she rooted through her purse to find the key. The pool of artificial moonlight from the street lamp cast scant illumination on the porch.

She could have sworn she'd left the exterior light on. But maybe she'd forgotten, or perhaps the bulb had burned out.

Her resolve faltered before she slid the key into the lock. She felt something, heard something like the hiss of a snake slipping through dry leaves. A slithery sensation raised goose bumps down her spine. At some intuitive level she knew there was someone, or something, on the other side of the heavy double doors. Waiting for her. *An aberrant force.* She tried to talk herself out of the feeling, out of a suddenly overactive imagination.

Lightning sheeted from one cloud to another, illuminating the dark corners of the porch. An instant later, a blue-green glow appeared at the bottom of the doorway, and she caught a cloyingly sweet odor, the scent of too many fading flowers . . . the perfume of funerals and death.

The glow beneath the door flared more brightly. Menacingly.

In a panic, she whirled and ran. Uncontrollable, irrational fear gripped her; a scream locked in her throat. Her high heels tattooed a staccato beat on the tile steps as she ran onto the sidewalk. In her mind she saw a long line of corpses laid out in rows one after the other, all of them decaying in the melting heat like sickeningly fragrant candle wax.

She fought back the bile that rose in her throat.

No way was she going into that building in the dark of night.

Suddenly, a car raced toward her from the main boulevard. Its lights blinded her, and she raised her arm to ward off the glare. Careening to her side of the street, the vehicle bumped up over the curb and braked to a stop only feet in front of her, effectively blocking the route to her car.

Fresh panic seized her. A woman alone on the streets at night was vulnerable. At risk of meeting all kinds of harm.

She turned back toward the mortuary. But she couldn't seek safety there, she thought frantically. Not when she knew something lurked on the other side of the door, waiting for her. And there was no help for her out here. At this late hour, the streets of old downtown Torrance were empty as a mausoleum.

Footsteps echoed close behind her.

"Hey, lady. Ease up." A large, very masculine hand snared her by the upper arm. "I'm not going to hurt you. I'm a cop."

Her head snapped around and her gaze met eyes that were so uncommonly light in color, they looked silver in the glow from the streetlight. She caught a whiff of polished leather, gun oil and a scent that could only be described as male sexuality. Margo tried to catch her breath. "Officer?"

"What's happening? Why were you running?"

"The mortuary...I thought..."

His features hardened and his fingers closed almost painfully around her arm. She stifled an urge to pull away. He was a big man, better than six feet, she guessed, broad-shouldered, and strong enough to break a person's neck with his bare hands, if he were so inclined. His uniform and the shiny badge over his left pocket looked impossibly intimidating. "What about the mortuary?" he asked. His lips settled into a grim line.

"I was letting myself in the door when I...I felt something." More than that. Terror had set in and her imagination had added color to her fear. "I know that sounds ridiculous—"

"Wait for me by the patrol car," he ordered in a voice that demanded obedience. "Don't budge an inch till I get back."

Without another word he was gone. Running in a crouched position, he took the porch steps two at a time, tried the locked door, then silently slid like a phantom into the shadows alongside the building. Margo strained, listening for his movements, but the only sounds she heard were an irregular ticking as the patrol car's engine cooled, crickets chirping in the sparsely landscaped curb area, and the distant hum of traffic on the boulevard. Farther away, a siren wailed and was answered by the low rumble of retreating thunder.

Sweat beaded her forehead and crept between her breasts as she edged her way to the patrol car and stood by the passenger door. The headlights reflected off a whitewashed wall with a glare that made her squint. The officer hadn't called for backup, she realized. That would be the standard operating procedure before he checked out a prowler... or whatever she had seen. Yet this cop was acting on his own. She wondered why.

Maybe she should pick up the mike tucked under the dashboard and call for assistance herself. But that would make the cop look bad to his boss. She didn't want to cause any trouble for a guy who had stopped to help.

Instead, she kept her attention riveted on the starkly white mortuary.

From the corner of her eye she caught the glimmer of a light in an upstairs room of the building. A reflection of lightning, she told herself. Or maybe the flash of car lights from the boulevard.

She rubbed her hands along her upper arms against a sudden chill. Lightning and headlights weren't tinged blue-green.

"Everything looks okay from the outside."

She whipped around at the sound of his deep, raspy voice right behind her, tipping her head back to look into his silver eyes. Half of his face was illuminated by the patrol car's headlights, and she noted the dark shadow of his evening beard across the rugged angle of his jaw. His hair was equally black except for a few threads of gray visible in his sideburns.

"Doors all locked," he added. "No broken windows."

She suppressed the unbidden thought that whatever she had seen and felt didn't bother using doors. "Thank you for checking."

"Now tell me why in hell you were trying to get into an abandoned mortuary in the middle of the night."

"I live here. It's my job." But not tonight, she reminded herself. Not a chance.

Skepticism pressed his heavy eyebrows into a dark line. "Your job? Nobody's lived in this place for nearly thirty years."

"That's about to change. The city is opening a shelter for homeless women and their children." A project she'd worked on for six months. Except for the fact she'd lobbied for the city to use the old hotel down the street, she would have been ecstatic.

He muttered a curse under his breath. "Yeah, I heard about the shelter. But you don't exactly look homeless to me."

Looks could be deceiving, she thought wryly. "I'm the on-site manager, starting now for the remodeling phase. That ought to last three to four months. I moved my things in this morning." She wished he weren't standing quite so close. Because of his size and muscular physique, he had an uncanny ability to slip inside her personal space. But she didn't step back. In recent years, refusing to back down to any man had become a matter of pride.

She studied his name tag. "I appreciate your help, Officer Rainer, but I think maybe I'll pull my car into the driveway and sleep there tonight. In the morning, I'll—"

"I can't let you do that."

She blinked. "I beg your pardon?"

"I can't let you sleep in your car. There's a city ordinance against it. Besides, it isn't safe."

At the moment, the mortuary didn't exactly feel like a safe haven, either. She'd as soon take her chances in a locked car. "It's only for a few hours," she told him. "You could look the other way this one time."

"Nope. Can't do that."

She speared her fingers through her hair in a weary gesture of frustration. "And just where would you propose I stay as an alternative?" She'd already given up the one-room apartment she'd called home for the last few months.

"There are motels around."

"The city must be paying you more than they pay me. Motel expenses aren't exactly a part of my budget, Officer Rainer."

"Kane. My name's Kane. With a *K*."

"Margo Stafford," she automatically responded, extending her hand. Lord, his hand was big, his palm roughly textured. Like a coal miner's, she imagined, or an Iowa farmer's.

"How 'bout calling a friend to take you in?"

"At this time of night, does anybody have a friend like that?"

He seemed to hesitate a moment, weighing some major decision while he held her hand a heartbeat too long. "You could stay at my place."

Her eyes widened at the softly spoken invitation, and she withdrew her hand.

Gesturing over his shoulder, he said, "I live there, second house from the corner. The place with the porch light on. I was coming off duty when I saw you running."

"I really don't think that's a good plan."

"There's an extra bedroom. It's not much but the sheets are clean. I'll check out the mortuary for you in the morning."

Margo got the distinct impression this wasn't a come-on. He seriously didn't want her to stay anywhere near the mortuary tonight. Nor did she relish the idea, she admitted as a low rumble of thunder brought a new line of storm clouds closer. For whatever reason, she had no fear of going home with Officer Kane Rainer. In fact, the opposite was the case. His presence made her feel safe. Tonight she needed that. Adrenaline was still coursing through her veins and, in truth, she'd been too badly spooked to want to be alone.

"I don't even have a toothbrush," she protested with a minimum of conviction.

"I keep a new one on hand for emergencies, and you can sleep in one of my T-shirts." He pulled open the passenger door of the patrol car and cupped her elbow. "Come on. Let's go."

Cops in uniform were a very persuasive breed, Margo concluded as she found herself being helped into the car. She could just as easily have walked the short distance across the street from the mortuary to his house. The sound of the door locks sliding into place made her heart leap. She didn't like the feeling she'd just been arrested for loitering after curfew.

Or worse yet, that she was locked inside a car with a man she had just met who had her imagination already racing.

With considerable willpower, she forced her pulse to slow to a normal beat.

Kane's house was a bungalow built about 1920, wood siding, asphalt-shingled roof, with low bushes across the front of the porch and a neatly trimmed lawn. The rest of the houses along the residential street were dark, typical of a Friday night in a part of town where the average age was seventy-plus and only a few of the homes housed young families with children.

He let Margo get out of the vehicle before he drove into the single-car garage. "Against the rules to park a patrol car on the street overnight," he said by way of explanation. "Too easy a target for vandals."

"I'm surprised you're allowed to bring the car home at all."

"I handle some special assignments."

She waited while he parked the car and carefully locked the garage. Then he ushered her into the house via the back door.

Except for an added dishwasher, the kitchen probably hadn't changed much since the house was built— a stand-alone gas range, painted wooden cabinets, a linoleum floor that had lost its shine. But the bright yellow walls, a few dishes on the tile counter and the Formica table in one corner of the room managed to create a sense of homeyness.

"Like I said, it isn't much." He unbuckled his gun belt and slid the revolver into a drawer by the back door. The way he handled it, she knew the weapon was heavy. Dangerous. Like the man.

"It's fine. Cozy." Feeling awkward, she stood in the middle of the small room clutching her suit jacket and purse. She'd never before gone home with a man. At least, no man except her husband. *Ex-husband,* she mentally corrected.

Loosening the top couple of buttons on his dark uniform shirt, he gazed at her from across the room. Self-consciously she tried not to meet his eyes, and in the process her attention slipped to his broad chest. He was wearing a heavy vest. Bullet-proof probably. A man ready to meet danger, she realized with a start that snapped her gaze back to his face.

In the light from the overhead fixture she saw his eyes weren't silver, but an extremely light blue, the color of a pale summer sky in the muggy heat of July. His expression was completely unreadable, giving her an unsettled feeling in the pit of her stomach.

"You want a beer?" Opening the aging refrigerator, he retrieved two bottles.

"No, I don't think so. It's been a long day."

"Coffee?"

She shook her head.

He put one bottle back and twisted the cap off the other, taking a long swig. "I'll show you your room."

"I appreciate your hospitality."

"No problem."

His broad shoulders nearly filled the narrow hallway that led to the back of the house; his hips were lean. He walked like a man who was comfortable with his body.

"My folks died a few years back," he said as he reached into a bedroom to flip the wall switch. There were bunk beds in the room, a matching maple chest of drawers and a Torrance High pennant on the wall. "I inherited the house. It's where I grew up. The john's at the end of the hall. I'll put towels out."

"I could use a shower."

"Go ahead. After finishing my shift, I usually sit around for a while. Too keyed up to sleep." His silver-blue gaze slipped over her in measured perusal. "My T-shirt's gonna be way too big."

Heat crept up Margo's neck. "It'll be fine."

Nodding, he turned and stepped into the room across the hall. The master bedroom, she surmised from the glimpse she caught of the big double bed with its rumpled bedding. A moment later he was back and he handed her a folded white T-shirt. The corners of his mouth twitched into a half smile. For the first time, she noticed he had very sensual lips.

"Guess I'm not real well equipped to handle female houseguests," he said.

"I don't have any complaints." In fact, she rather liked the idea that women didn't normally drop by unexpectedly at Kane's house for an overnight stay. It made her feel a little less as though she'd entered the den of a potentially dangerous predator.

He wasn't a messy guy, but not a neatnik, either. The teal blue towels that matched the throw rug were carefully hung, the sink was mostly clean and his shaving gear was arranged conveniently on the counter.

Margo smiled to herself. She remembered how her dad had used a safety razor, and how she'd loved to watch him stroke the lather from his weather-worn cheeks in one clean stripe after another. Then he'd twisted his lips so he could get the last of his whiskers from around his mouth and under his nose. She hadn't thought about that in years.

Gingerly she lifted the can of Kane's shaving foam, squirted a bit onto her fingertips and sniffed. It had to be the same spicy soap as her father had used.

Kane had evidently grown up in this house, she mused. It was pretty commonplace in the Midwest for generations to live one after the other in the same place. It seemed odd the same thing could happen in a suburban area like Torrance.

Setting thoughts of Kane and memories of her father aside, she rinsed out her panty hose and hung them to dry. Moments later, she shed her clothes and stepped into the shower.

He'd kept Margo Stafford safe for one night, but what the hell was he going to do for tomorrow?

Kane tossed the empty beer bottle into the recycling sack in the broom closet, then rummaged through the refrigerator for a second beer. The lady was definitely a class act, he'd give her that. She walked and talked like one of those snooty folks who lived behind the guarded gates up on the Palos Verdes Peninsula. Even the car she drove, the old Caddie parked by the curb at the mortuary, looked like wealth. Probably a do-gooder set on saving the world, down here slumming with the homeless.

He'd met women like that. When you pulled them over for speeding, or running a red light, they acted as if they owned the whole damn world, instead of thinking you might have just saved their life—or someone else's.

In the living room, he switched on the TV, not bothering to check the program. The shower was running, and it was too damn easy to imagine the lady with water sluicing over her naked body. She wasn't very big. Maybe five-two. Breasts that would each be a comfortable handful. Hair cut in a casual style that skimmed her shoulders and softly framed her classic features in a halo of golden brown, the shade of summer-dry grass on the hills outside of L.A. He suspected that under the right circumstances her hazel eyes could turn to icy blue, or fill with the green depths of passion...

A sudden jolt of fear snapped him out of his reverie. Nobody would listen to him about the Miller Mortuary. For more than twenty-five years he'd been trying to tell them there was something deadly in that place. Now, unless he could come up with a plan, the city would finally have reason to believe him. But by then it would be too damn late for Margo Stafford.

Unless, God help him, he'd been the one to blame all along.

Can't catch me! Neener-neener. Can't catch meee. The shrill, singsong voice in Kane's head taunted him with memories so sharp his hands clenched into lethal fists.

Margo Stafford didn't deserve to die.

CHAPTER TWO

She woke from the dream drenched in sweat. Bodies. Dozens of them. Grinning obscenely at her.

Dragging in a steadying breath, Margo stared up at the bunk bed over her head. Chiseled into the first pine slat was a single word: *KILLER.*

"Oh, God," she groaned. A kid's prank, she told herself as she hastily rolled out of bed. Little boys did that sort of thing, carved initials and ugly words into any bit of wood they could find. Particularly macho boys who grew up to be cops.

Kane Rainer wasn't a killer. If he were, her throat would be slashed by now. And everyone would know how foolish she'd been to go home with a total stranger, cop or not.

With a shake of her head, she tried to rid herself of morbid thoughts. The mortuary was getting to her. It was only an empty building, she reminded herself. No more, no less. Not something that should be giving her nightmares or sending her imagination into high gear. No spooks, no skeletons, no eerie lights. It was all in her head.

Outside, knobby tropical storm clouds—pushed north from Mexico—streaked the dawn sky and promised another day of record October heat. But, for now, the morning air was comfortably cool.

An early riser by nature, Margo assumed a guy who worked swing shift would be the opposite. It was just as well. She wasn't quite ready to face her host.

Hoping to cleanse her mind of the nightmare, she made her way to the living room. Kane had left an empty beer bottle on the coffee table next to a current copy of a collector-car magazine. The CDs on the stereo suggested he favored country-western music with a little soft rock mixed in. His limited video collection featured *Star Wars* one and two, along with a complete collection of "Star Trek" shows. A man with basic, down-to-earth kinds of tastes, she surmised.

Picking up the empty beer bottle, she carried it to the kitchen, found a sack of empties in a narrow closet, then returned to the living room. During the still moments that followed dawn, before the roar of traffic raised the ambient noise level, she would take time for her morning ritual.

She picked a spot in front of an overstuffed chair, opposite a small brick fireplace, and sat cross-legged on the floor, pulling Kane's T-shirt down over her knees. As she closed her eyes to facilitate her daily meditations, she was oddly aware of the softness of his shirt and the faint winter-green scent of soap in the fabric.

A few minutes later, the swish of denim brushing against denim interrupted her concentration.

She opened her eyes to discover Kane standing at the arched entrance to the hallway. He'd tugged on a pair of faded jeans that rode low on his hips, pulled tautly across his pelvis and gloved his muscular thighs. Bare from the waist up, dark hair covered his broad chest in soft swirls.

A sudden rush of sexual awareness jolted Margo. The sensation was so unexpected—so unfamiliar—she almost failed to recognize the heated feeling that curled low through her body. Her breath lodged in her lungs.

"You okay?" he asked, his voice morning rough as he spoke his first words of the day.

"I'm fine." Except her blood seemed to be rushing from her head to her nether regions, and her mouth had gone uncharacteristically dry.

"Do you always prefer the floor over a chair?"

"Only when I'm meditating."

"Ah," he drawled, strolling into the room, his thumbs hooked in his pockets, his hands unconsciously forming an erotic frame displaying the worn zipper on his jeans to best advantage. "That's what you're doing."

She swallowed a groan. He wasn't a killer. It simply wasn't possible, except perhaps a "lady killer."

"Don't make fun unless you've tried it."

"I'm game." He lifted his shoulders in an easy gesture of unconcern.

"Now?"

"Why not?" Shoving the coffee table aside, he sat down opposite her. Dark whiskers shadowed his features and amusement sparked in his silver-blue eyes. "Looks like a whole lot of fun."

"It's supposed to help you focus on your goals. For instance, I'm clearing my mind so I can concentrate on getting the homeless shelter open." And forget about the persistently eerie feelings she got whenever she went near the mortuary. *Bodies. Death. That ugly floral scent.*

A frown tugged his eyebrows flat.

"Meditating isn't that hard to do," she assured him. Except today her concentration seemed to be split. Kane's mussed hair drew part of her attention, wayward locks she wanted to finger-comb into place, while at the same time she kept remembering the carved accusation. *KILLER.* "Just rest your hands, palms up, on your knees. Relax them like this," she instructed.

He did as she asked. "Got it."

His fingernails were neatly manicured, his hands big and powerful like the rest of his body. Potentially dangerous. Possibly gentle.

"Now close your eyes," she said, a slight quiver in her voice, "and picture a yellow ball of energy circling around you."

"Like a yellow tennis ball?" he asked.

"No, more like a miniature sun. Very powerful." And radiating heat. Like you.

Kane tried to concentrate on what she was saying, but failed. In his experience, people who were into things like meditation had their feet firmly planted in midair. They were either slightly nutso, or downright innocent. He figured Margo fit into the latter category.

Not that she was all that young—around thirty, he guessed. But she was vulnerable in the way people who hadn't experienced the hard knocks of life were, those who hadn't battled the hoods on the street. She'd expect the best, be shattered when the worst happened. He'd seen it before, particularly in women who couldn't handle the stress of being married to a cop.

Still, he felt something shift and rearrange itself deep in his gut, like the snapping in place of an automatic's clip, and he knew he had to find a way to protect this woman. He hoped to God *he* wasn't the one she needed protection from.

Just as well he was determined not to let his relationship with Margo Stafford get personal.

He'd made a fair number of mistakes in his thirty-nine years. Giving Margo one of his white T-shirts to wear rated right up there with jumping off the garage roof with homemade wings strapped to his back. Both errors in judgment brought him a lot of pain.

Obviously the lady wasn't wearing a bra. The faint shadow of her nipples was visible every time she shifted her position. That realization gave him a pain, unlike his flying fiasco, that was pretty darn specific to his groin area.

Closing her eyes, Margo said, "Think of a ball of energy moving slowly around your head. Give it a count of five to cover the distance, then let it drift lower, always slowly circling, and you can feel yourself centering."

"Centering? Where did you learn this stuff?"

She opened her eyes. He wasn't meditating. His body was too stiff, too rigidly alert, too much like a predator about to pounce. His eyes were focused on her lips. Instinctively, she licked them and swallowed.

With minute precision, his gaze followed the movement of her tongue.

She swallowed hard. "At the library."

"You spend a lot of time there?"

"It's a good place to study." The library was also warm and dry and safe when you didn't have anywhere else to go. "I just finished my bachelor's degree in June—Human Services. When things settle down at the mortuary—the shelter—I hope to find time to work on my master's. Eventually, I'd like to be a licensed counselor." Though it might take years, she realized.

A nod of what appeared to be approval acknowledged her statement. He studied her a moment longer, his gaze so intense his eyes darkened to a shade much deeper than usual, much more primordial, and Margo felt her flesh warm.

"You ready for coffee?" he asked.

"Sure." Lord, she was ready to put a whole lot of distance between herself and Kane Rainer. She didn't imagine for a second the man would appreciate the erotic thoughts his nearness conjured up in her suddenly fertile imagination. Perhaps the fear she'd experienced last night had colored her perception of Kane in the light of day.

He moved around the kitchen with an economy of motion, filling the filter with coffee, adding water to the pot, pouring two glasses of orange juice. Having accomplished the preliminaries, he vanished down the hall for a minute and returned wearing a raspberry-red T-shirt sporting the logo of a 10K run. The Human Race, Margo mused, reading the stencil. He was definitely a superior specimen.

"Cereal okay with you?" he asked.

"Anything's fine." She paused, then added, "I thought you'd sleep later."

"I don't require much sleep," he said. "If I feel tired later, I can take a nap before my shift." He placed a couple of boxes of cereal on the table, bowls and a carton of milk. By now the coffee was ready. He filled two mugs. "How do you take it?"

"Black."

He glanced across the room at her. "You're easy to get along with."

"I hate to impose on anyone."

"You're not."

They settled down opposite each other at the small table and ate in silence for a while. Out on the street, cars drove by, a horn honked and that started a dog barking. Somewhere a baby cried. A mostly quiet Saturday morning in a mostly quiet neighborhood. Margo envied the stable, peaceful life Kane lived. Odd she'd think that, when a cop must surely be constantly on guard, and often faced with moments of stark terror.

He rested his spoon in his empty bowl. "Margo, I want you to tell me what happened last night."

At the seriousness of his tone, she flashed on the raw panic she'd experienced. "At the mortuary?" He nodded. "I'm not sure. Maybe it was just the storm that spooked me."

"You don't believe that any more than I do. I want you to tell me everything you saw. Even if you're not sure it was real."

She fought the knot that formed in her stomach. She didn't want to remember, not the feelings, not the awful images of dead bodies. She had to live in that building, for God's sake, and she didn't want to think about how she'd survive staying there alone for the time it took to remodel the place. At least after it opened, the sound of voices and laughter and plans being made would fill the eerie silence.

"I can't help if you don't tell me what went on," he insisted when she didn't respond.

"Well, I . . . I went up onto the porch to let myself in. It was dark and I had to fumble in my purse for the key. I really thought I'd left the exterior light on. . . ." Unwilling to meet his eyes, she concentrated on the task of folding a paper napkin into a tiny square as she spoke. "Anyway, I found my key and started to slip it into the lock. That's when I felt . . . It sounds so stupid now, but I thought there was something . . . unnatural on the other side of the door." She glanced up to catch his reaction.

"Unnatural?" he questioned, his expression revealing nothing at all.

"You know, like a demon, or maybe some lost soul—a ghost—who had been left behind at the mortuary when its body went off in the hearse to the cemetery." Great, she thought, now he was going to think she was crazy. She rubbed her temple, a stress headache threatening. She'd never believed in ghosts and things that went bump in the night. Why now? she wondered. And would Kane decide a woman who meditated was also given to wild flights of fancy?

To her surprise, as though he accepted her story at face value, Kane didn't blink at her references to the supernatural. "Okay. What else?"

"I thought I saw...maybe it had something to do with the electrical storm."

"What?" he persisted as though interrogating a suspect.

"At the bottom of the door, I saw..." Her hands began to tremble and she squeezed her napkin into a ball. In her imagination she smelled again the cloying scent of thousands of decaying flowers. "There was a blue-green glow and it seemed to... It was coming after me. Or at least that's what I thought. And that's when I ran."

"This glow you're talking about was attacking you?"

She nodded. "You probably think I'm crazy."

"No, I don't."

"Why not?" she asked incredulously. "If I went to my boss at city hall with this kind of a cockamamy story, he'd probably send me to the local shrink, or fire me on the spot."

"Yeah, well, maybe he hasn't lived around here as long as I have." Kane shoved back his chair and stood. "You make yourself at home. I'm going to go check out the mortuary."

"I'm coming with you."

"You'd be safer here."

"I'm going to live in that building. I've been inside before, more than once, and I'm going to have to get used to the place sooner or later." In the daylight it had only seemed creepy; the nights were what worried her.

He leaned over and splayed his hands on the breakfast table, bringing his face close to hers. A muscle rippled at his whisker-shadowed jaw. "Lady, if you were smart, you'd quit your job."

Lifting her chin with stubborn bravado, she returned his steely gaze. "I can't quit."

Their eyes locked in a silent battle of wills.

"Suit yourself," he finally said.

Margo dressed, and before they left the house, Kane tucked a gun in the waistband of his jeans and pulled his T-shirt down to disguise the telltale bulge. The sight of the weapon sent a new surge of fear through Margo's midsection. What did he expect to find at the mortuary?

With every step closer to the mortuary, her anxiety increased and the morning heat grew in intensity, making sweat gather along her hairline. Irrational fear, she told herself, only her vivid imagination conjuring up images of a long line of pale, gray bodies that had rested briefly in the building. The structure could serve other purposes just as well, wood and stucco that would now provide shelter for the living, not the dead.

She walked quickly to keep up with Kane's long-legged stride, her high heels clicking on the asphalt. Strange, she mused, that he so willingly accepted her story of threatening blue-green lights. His whole attitude suggested he knew there was something not quite right about the Miller Mortuary. A curious man indeed.

So curious, she realized, that as a boy he'd carved the word *KILLER* on a bed slat right above his head. She wondered why.

"It looked to me like somebody took a Boy Scout knife to the bunk bed."

Kane slanted her a look. As realization dawned that she was talking about the carving, his eyes narrowed. "That wasn't my doing. My kid brother, Albert. He was always trying to get me in trouble with our folks. More times than not, it worked. In this case, it was ... prophetic."

The hard-edged abruptness of Kane's response didn't invite further questions, and Margo wasn't sure she wanted to know the answer, anyway. Her nerves were already skittering around like a drop of ice water on a sizzling frying pan.

Fortunately, by then they'd reached the double oak doors of the mortuary.

Kane extended his hand for the key. "You can wait out here if you want."

"No. This is my job we're talking about. If there's something in there..." She left the thought unfinished. Nothing in her background had prepared her to deal with a supernatural force, if that's what she'd been feeling. She doubted Kane had taken a course on the subject at the police academy, or anywhere else. As far as she could tell, they were both flying blind. That was *not* a reassuring thought.

He didn't look pleased with her decision to enter the mortuary, but he proceeded to open the door.

The moment she stepped inside, the short hairs at the back of Margo's neck prickled for no apparent reason. There weren't any ghosts, no mysterious glow. Only the musty smell of disuse and a mountain of harmless dust balls. At least that's what her intelligent mind registered.

But at some far more basic level, she knew she and Kane were not entirely alone.

Fear parched her throat. "Do you feel it?" she asked.

"I don't deal in feelings, Ms. Stafford. *Facts* are my stock and trade."

He stood immobile in the middle of the vestibule. Listening, she thought. All Margo could hear was blood pounding through her heart.

A stained-glass window rose from the floor to the top of the cathedral ceiling, casting variegated colors across the worn carpeting—rose red, daffodil yellow, leaves of green, each shade outlined in a thin thread of black. In this area of the building, Margo would arrange reception and counseling for new arrivals to the shelter, and set up a hot-line telephone service for women in crisis. That was her job. She was going to be damn good at it. She had to be.

When Kane headed into the spacious chapel, Margo followed. She tried not to think about the word *KILLER,* or corpses and caskets and grieving families. Or why there had been such pain in Kane's voice when he spoke about his brother.

"Half of this room will be set up as a dormitory facility for single women," she said, as much to hear her own voice as to explain the proposed operation to Kane. "The rest of the space will accommodate recreational activities, child care and occupational programs. What used to be the private family-mourning room will be our TV room."

Kane grunted a noncommittal sound. He checked every closet and cupboard and peered out a side door into what used to be a garage for the hearse, first horse-drawn and later gasoline-powered. The floor of the garage was dirt and the room carried the residual smell of oil and gasoline.

"What about the rest of the rooms on this floor?"

"The viewing rooms? We'll turn those into offices, plus a shower and laundry room for transients."

"Why can't they go to the Laundromat like the rest of us?" he muttered, heading toward the rooms she had described.

"They don't have any money, Kane. That's why they're homeless." She hurried after him. Sympathy for the homeless did not appear to be Kane's long suit. Maybe if she could get him involved in some of the shelter activities, she could turn him around. After all, they were going to be neighbors, in a manner of speaking. And, she admitted, she'd like an excuse to see him from time to time. Not that she expected him to reciprocate the feeling.

"I thought welfare was supposed to take care of these people." He opened the door to a small rest room, glanced inside, then closed it again.

"Sometimes it does. But it takes a while to get the first check after you apply, and then it's tough to save up first and last months' rent. With one little glitch in her support system, it's easy for a woman to find herself living on the street."

He didn't appear convinced.

After thoroughly checking out the first floor, they made their way upstairs.

"This is it?" he asked, his gaze scanning her personal quarters with less than hearty approval. "This is where you're going to be living?"

"One room will be my office, the other my bedroom." Granted, she wasn't thrilled with the prospect, either. And it certainly didn't look like much with only a few scattered pieces of furniture and a dozen boxes stacked helter-skelter. But it was a place to stay, four walls and a roof. She had definitely learned to appreciate the basics. Added to that, she had a steady job at a reasonable salary with an automatic raise due at the end of her probationary period. Surely, in time, the creepy feeling of living in a mortuary would go away.

She sat on a box, slipped off her high heels and slid her feet into a pair of flats she took from a nearby box. With a silent groan, she rubbed her ankle where it was tender from a prior injury. ''There's a kitchen that all of the residents will use, the house manager included. That's one of the biggest remodeling projects we'll have to do. For now, I'll manage with a small microwave.''

He walked through her two rooms, his fingers brushing a box here, the back of a chair there, until he stood before a locked cupboard about three feet above the floor.

''What's in here?''

''I don't know. Probably nothing. I haven't been able to come up with a key yet.''

''You should get a locksmith.''

''It hasn't seemed important.'' Some doors, she sensed, shouldn't be opened too eagerly.

''Do it. Soon.''

She bristled. The guy should be a drill sergeant, not a street cop. He was too bossy by far. ''When I have a chance,'' she said, enunciating each word carefully between clenched teeth.

''I'll arrange it.''

Before she could sputter any further objection, he'd marched out of the room and headed down the stairs. Fuming, she caught up with him at the door to the basement. She'd avoided inspecting this part of the building till now, sensing it was a dark, dank place she really didn't want to be. But Kane didn't hesitate. And dammit, this was *her* job. She couldn't very well let him go down there alone.

Now this was spooky, she thought, creeping down the steep stairs right behind him. The light switch hadn't worked, because of a circuit problem or for lack of a functioning bulb, she couldn't be sure. So except for a rectangle of light that filtered in through the open door, it was dark. Really dark. And it stank of dust and mildew and an acrid scent of rotten vegetation . . . flowers grown old and wilted.

"What did they do down here?" she asked, gagging on the smells.

"Embalmed the bodies."

Margo shuddered and grabbed a handful of the back of Kane's shirt.

He switched on a penlight that didn't do much to press back the darkness. "It's okay. There's nothing here now."

"Do you think someone was here last night?"

He flashed the light upward at the ceiling where water pipes crisscrossed the basement in ugly, galvanized strips. Cobwebs thick with dust dangled here and there in the surreal shadows, looking like dirty skeins of green-gray silk. "Possibly someone. Possibly some*thing*."

That *wasn't* what she wanted to hear.

The man talked in riddles, forget she'd had similar thoughts.

The slender column of light slid across the floor and settled on a small mound in the corner.

"What's that?" she asked.

"Don't know." He walked across the room, Margo still clinging to his shirt, and poked at the indecipherable mass with his toe. Dust rose, along with the scent of decay. "Rodents. Dead ones," he said succinctly.

"Rats?" Her voice caught on the question.

"Looks like."

"Why would they invade an abandoned mortuary? There isn't anything here for them to eat."

"Maybe they were gnawing on the electrical insulation. Hard to know."

"Let's get out of here," she pleaded, her stomach threatening rebellion. She was tired of straining to make sense out of ugly watermarks on the walls of the basement, dead rats and a concrete floor serpentined with cracks. The city building-and-safety people would have to handle this part of the job. She didn't intend to set foot in the basement again if she could avoid it.

By the time they returned to the vestibule, the sunlight had shifted, the stained-glass window now slashing the carpeting with splotches of blood red and bilious green. What had once seemed benign, even pretty, appeared gruesome in the shifting pattern of light and dark.

A tremor of apprehension fluttered down Margo's spine.

Thorough man that he was, Kane left to check the roof for any signs of illegal entry. Since he was going to shimmy up drain spouts and clamber over walls without the help of a ladder, Margo elected to wait for him on the porch. The oppressive heat of the day was already beginning to gather inside the stucco building, and the vestibule suddenly lacked a welcoming appeal. At least outside a slight sea breeze provided some small measure of relief from the heat.

Kane was definitely obsessive about the mortuary, she decided. He'd checked every crack and cranny. There was absolutely no sign of a break-in. In fact, it seemed almost odd that vagrants or vandals hadn't targeted this abandoned building a long time ago. The nearby state employment office always attracted a fair share of those who were down-and-out. Funny they hadn't commandeered the mortuary for their own.

Then again, with Kane living so close, maybe word had spread he wouldn't tolerate trespassers. He'd certainly been ready to run her off in a hurry last night. For which she'd been grateful, of course.

Even so, as she thought about his behavior, she wondered if she was being foolish to trust Kane so completely. Cops could be crooks, too. Or eccentric, she supposed. Even killers. In any case, she might be well-advised to keep a wary eye on Kane Rainer.

"Young lady! Young lady, we want to talk to you."

Margo looked up to see a middle-aged man and an elderly woman coming toward her. A dog resembling a waddling dust mop, all shaggy fur and no eyes, preceded them along the sidewalk, tugging on its leash.

"Hello, Mrs. Cornelius," Margo said, recognizing the downtown busybody from her appearances at city council meetings where she'd protested the opening of the homeless shelter. Rumor had it she was planning to run for city council and had a good chance of getting elected. She might well be a pain in the rear, but she was also very influential.

"Are you having trouble already?" the older woman asked. Tall and angular, Bernice Cornelius was all skin and bones and wrinkles, and had a voice like a sliding door that didn't quite fit properly in its groove.

"We were told, young lady, that no one would occupy the mortuary for some time." Mrs. Cornelius's companion, Walter Wiengold, neighborhood veterinarian, had been equally adamant in his opposition to the shelter. "We won't have you city people rushing things. We want to know what's going on."

The dog sniffed around Margo's shoe.

"There's really nothing to worry about, Dr. Wiengold. To see that the project goes forward smoothly, I'm going to be in residence during the entire remodeling phase." Margo gave them the official city story, wondering if she'd really be able to live here the necessary three or four months without having a nervous breakdown.

"We saw that boy Kane poking around up on the roof," Mrs. Cornelius said.

"Boy?" Margo suppressed a smile. Perhaps Bernice Cornelius needed a new pair of glasses to replace the wire-rimmed contraption that rested at the end of her beaked nose.

"You know who we mean. He never has been quite right, you know, not since he was a boy," Mrs. Cornelius announced. "Bad genes, I suppose. You can see it in his eyes. Peculiar, they are. Something not quite right about that boy. Something dangerous."

KILLER. The word fairly shrieked through Margo's mind before she could suppress it. *A prophetic carving.* She swallowed hard. "Really, Mrs. Cornelius," Margo said, doing the best she could to rationalize her confused feelings, "Kane is an officer on the Torrance police force. I hardly think the city would hire a man who was dangerous to anyone except criminals."

The veterinarian shook his head. "You're new in town and didn't grow up with Kane like I did. There are things you simply don't know."

"Odd things." The would-be member of city council shook her finger right in Margo's face. "And you'd be smart to keep your distance, young lady. Kane Rainer has always meant trouble."

Ignored by its owner, the dog pawed at Margo's shoe and she yanked her foot away.

"I'll certainly keep your advice in mind, Mrs. Cornelius."

"See that you do. As for the shelter, don't be so sure it's actually going to open, miss. We still hope the city council will see they have made a terrible mistake that just might cost them the next election. It's simply not right to have this kind of a facility—those people—in our nice quiet part of town."

"Please, Mrs. Cornelius, won't you and the doctor give us a chance—give women who don't have anywhere else to go a chance for a new start. Once we open, I'd really like you both to meet some of the clients, get to know them as people. I'm sure—"

"I think not!" Mrs. Cornelius said with conviction. "Our neighborhood will not welcome *street people.*"

Before Margo could respond, she felt something warm and wet trickle across her foot. Her stomach threatening revolt, she grimaced.

"Mrs. Cornelius," she said carefully, afraid she'd lose her temper and all chance of getting the neighborhood residents on the side of the homeless, "your dog just urinated on my foot."

"Oh, poor little Poopsie," the old woman crooned, kneeling beside her dog and petting her. "She's had the most terrible bladder infection, hasn't she, dear doctor? She didn't mean to do a naughty-naughty, did you, sweet'ums?"

Margo rolled her eyes.

"We may have to increase the dosage of the antibiotic," the vet suggested with a frown. "She is getting older, you know."

"Nonsense. She's just a baby."

"Nearly seventeen years old. You really can't expect—"

"Really, Walter, we ladies don't like our ages discussed in public."

"Is there something I can do for you folks?" At the sound of Kane's deep, resonant voice, all heads turned in his direction.

While his question might have been intended for the others, Kane's eyes focused on Margo. She felt absorbed by the pale blue silvery depths of them, by their energy and otherworldly heat. He was power, he was strength. She felt drawn to him as she had never been moved by another man. Whatever anyone else said, Kane could not possibly be a killer. She'd know. Surely she would.

When the others failed to respond, she forced herself to answer his question. "Mrs. Cornelius and the doctor were afraid we were having some problem."

"No problem," he responded bluntly without any elaboration. Forget the spooky things Margo had experienced, and the compulsive search of the building Kane had just completed. For these two neighbors, the answer was *No problem*.

Mrs. Cornelius scooped the dog into her arms as though Kane's presence might contaminate the dreadful little creature. "I trust you'll see it stays that way, young man. We don't want awful things happening again like they did when you were a child." She turned to Margo. "And you, miss, had best mark my words well. I'm warning you."

Margo shuddered as the two neighborhood busybodies hurried away as though on some mission of monumental importance.

"What did the ol' witch tell you?" Kane asked.

She shrugged off his concern. "Not much. Only that you'd always meant trouble and I should keep my distance."

His dark eyebrows formed a solid line and he nailed Margo with a look that took her breath away. "That's probably damn good advice."

His words sucked the breath from her as surely as if she'd been punched in the stomach. He'd put her in her place.

And it hurt, dammit! More than it should.

CHAPTER THREE

The shocked expression in Margo's trusting hazel eyes tore at Kane's gut, particularly since he'd heard her come to his defense only minutes ago. Not many people in the neighborhood would do that. He wondered if she discovered the truth—the dark secret Bernice and Walt could so easily reveal—would Margo bother to defend him the next time around.

Kane knew better than to get too close to Margo. He wasn't the kind of guy who could handle hearts and flowers. Yet he was beginning to care about her, and whether she knew it or not, she needed protection. He would simply have to keep her at arm's length.

If that was possible.

"What did you mean by that crack?" she asked, a slight tremor in her voice. "About me keeping my distance?"

"It isn't important."

She lifted her chin in an admirable display of stubborn pride. "I think it is."

Ignoring her comment, Kane said, "I'm going to check the electrical system. You said you were having trouble."

"It was probably a burned-out bulb on the porch. No big deal."

"It won't take me long."

"Fine. Go ahead, if that's what it takes to make you happy." She spat out the words. "I'm going upstairs to change and start unpacking. I'll keep out of your way."

"Margo!" He captured her by the arm. She was scared enough about staying at the mortuary. Now he'd hurt her, too. He hadn't meant for that to happen, and he cursed himself for being so thoughtless of her feelings. "I didn't mean to upset you."

"Of course not. You simply made yourself abundantly clear. You demonstrated your generosity by letting me stay at your place last night when I was in a dither over something as silly as an electrical storm. I appreciate that. I promise I won't bother you further, Officer Rainer."

"That's not what... You don't understand." But how could he make her understand without revealing too much about himself? Kane wondered.

With an imperious look, she glanced down at his fingers still wrapped around her arm. "If you'll excuse me?"

With a nod, he released her. What other choice did he have...besides telling her the truth and seeing questions form in her eyes? Questions that had no answers.

He jammed his hands into his pockets, fury at himself making him want to lash out. Why the hell couldn't he remember?

Margo hurried inside, kicked off her fouled shoes by the door to deal with them later and beat a speedy retreat up the stairs. She wasn't going to cry. She'd misread Kane, that was all. Just because she found him attractive didn't mean he reciprocated the feeling. Far from it. And because he'd been nice to her once didn't mean he wanted to hang around with her from now on.

She'd play it cool. She had a job to do, a darn important one, and she needed to get settled in. On Monday, the workmen would be here to start the remodeling, the phones would be installed, measurements taken, partitions aligned. There was a lot of work to be done between now and then.

She'd spent too much of her life afraid the dinner party she'd planned wouldn't meet with her husband's approval, or what she'd chosen to wear wouldn't be quite right. She wasn't going to waste any more time on fear...not fear of creepy things that glowed in the dark, or macabre images created by her fanciful imagination.

The corpses had all been removed years ago from the mortuary—along with their ghosts.

Tugging open an old, half-stuck window in her bedroom, she drew in a lungful of hot, humid air. If only the weather would cool off, she wouldn't feel so edgy. And achy, down deep where her loneliness festered like an open wound that she tried not to rub raw with her memories. Sometimes she failed. Like now. When Kane had made her think of impossible things she shouldn't even be considering.

She wasn't any great shakes when it came to sex appeal. Her marriage had taught her that. Among other unpleasant realities.

As she changed into shorts and a tank top, she eyed the locked cupboard beside her bed. Kane could issue orders all he liked, but she had better things to do than to spend her time searching for a key. Besides, the cupboard was likely as empty as the rest of the mortuary.

Hurrying downstairs, she opened more windows and a side door off a patio area that would someday serve as a children's play yard. She wanted to get rid of the musty scent of disuse in the building and replace it with the smell of hope and optimism. Positive affirmations. That's how she'd learned to survive one day at a time.

As she walked barefoot through the rooms, she noticed spots on the carpeting that seemed eerily warm, as if there was a hot-water pipe running directly beneath the floor. But that wasn't possible. She hadn't gotten the water heater turned back on yet, and had been dreading cold showers. Although, in this heat, she figured she'd find them refreshing.

On her inspection, she didn't see Kane. She didn't look. And she ignored the sense of foreboding Mrs. Cornelius's warning had created. *Dangerous. KILLER.*

Concentrating first on getting her bedroom into some semblance of order, she found the box she'd packed with her blankets and sheets. She'd feel more at home with somewhere of her own to sleep—not a borrowed bed in a stranger's house.

As she billowed the sheet across the mattress, a high-pitched sound stopped her—a scream of pain or the demented laugh of someone crazed, she couldn't be sure which. A gooseflesh tingle crept along her nape.

She held her breath. Listening.

The hysterical screech came again, strangely familiar now but no less frightening, this time with words. *Watch out! He'll kill you.*

She whirled and stared at the locked cupboard beside her bed. No more than three feet high, there couldn't be anyone inside. And how would they have gotten there in the first place? No one had the key. She'd already asked. And yet she'd heard…or maybe she'd only sensed …

Trying to maintain her calm, she frantically searched for answers.

Then she realized, on the opposite side of that wall was the … bathroom.

She almost collapsed in relief. What she'd heard had been water moving through old pipes. That had to be it. Nothing scary in that, she told herself. The whole building was likely to be filled with creaks and groans. Perfectly natural.

Except, she realized with a growing sense of panic, the unearthly noise she'd heard had been distinctly *inside* her head, not in the walls.

And that was utter nonsense.

Pulling the sheet taut, she noted her trembling hands. God, she was a nervous wreck. Her imagination had evidently taken flight.

She'd always prided herself on being very level-headed. Until recently.

An instant later, an explosive sound cut sharply through the silence of the mortuary.

Margo nearly jumped out of her skin.

"Dammit!" Kane bellowed from downstairs. His first curse was followed by a string of even more graphic expletives.

Fueled by an incredible surge of fear, Margo raced down the stairs. She found Kane standing by the outside fuse box. A worrisome ribbon of smoke drifted up from the metal case attached to the wall. But nothing awful had happened. No dead bodies. No arms or legs blown to smithereens. No gory corpse to discover.

"You okay?" she asked, trying to catch her breath, and calm her thundering heart. She could see by the way he was blowing on his palm that he'd probably burned himself.

"Yeah, sure. I'm fine."

"I gather things aren't going well."

He eyed Margo and then the blackened fuses. "Not exactly."

"You probably ought to run some cold water over your hand. It'll stop the pain."

"It's only a flash burn."

"Right." Men were all alike. If they weren't bleeding to death, they'd never admit to having any pain. Unless they had a sore throat, of course. Then they'd swear they were dying. "Come on. There's a drinking fountain in the vestibule. We'll use that."

With obvious reluctance, he followed her inside. As she ran the cold water over his hand, she tried not to think about how close they were standing, or how his size made her feel both feminine and extraordinarily vulnerable. *Dangerous*, Mrs. Cornelius had said. *Not quite right*. If only Margo could get those words out of her head.

"I guess my hands were sweaty," Kane explained. "The screwdriver slipped when I was prying off one of the fuses."

"Can the damage be fixed?"

"You'll need an electrician."

"I'll call the city. They'll send someone out."

"Not today they won't."

She raised her gaze to meet his silver-blue eyes, eyes that looked at her so steadily they didn't appear at all filled with remorse for messing up the electrical system. And that gave her a seriously uneasy feeling. "Why won't they come today? This is city property."

"It's Saturday, remember? It takes an act of God and the city manager's approval in quadruplicate to get someone authorized to work overtime."

"Oh, damn," she muttered. "I forgot."

"Sorry." The apology didn't quite ring true.

"Do I have *any* electricity?"

"I'm afraid I melted half the wires together. Everything's shorted. I'd say it will take a day or two to get things straightened out."

In dismay, she exhaled a long sigh. "Swell! Now what am I supposed to do? The workmen are due Monday. And where am I going to sleep in the meantime? I can't very well stay here in the dark." She was already on the verge of panic in the daylight. The night would be impossible without well-lit rooms to drive away morbid images and turn down the volume on the unearthly voices in her head.

With studied casualness, he wiped his palm on his jeans-clad thigh. "Guess you'll have to spend the night with me again."

"What?" Her voice rose in surprise. "Only an hour ago, you said—"

With belated awareness, she noted the stubborn angle of Kane's jaw, the determined look in his eyes and the way he stood his ground with his feet spread wide apart, like a man who was ready for anything. He wasn't the kind of guy who accidentally fused electrical wires together. He'd done it, she realized, on purpose.

"Why?" she asked incredulously. "Why did you do it?"

"Do what?" He failed to meet her eyes.

"Don't play coy with me, Kane. For some reason, you don't want me to stay in the mortuary. What do you know that I don't?"

At least he had the good sense to look sheepish, like a cop caught in a sting operation.

Glancing around the vestibule, as if someone might be listening, he said, "It's too hot to hang around here. Without power, we can't do much, anyway. Let's go down to the beach and cool off."

"I'm not going anywhere with you until you tell me what's going on. And what Bernice Cornelius meant when she warned me away from you."

He jammed his fingertips into his hip pockets. "Lock up. I'll tell you everything you want to know when we're at the beach."

The tropical storm lingering off the coast had kicked up the waves. They crashed against the King Harbor breakwater, sending salty plumes of spray into the air. A few intrepid fishermen were risking possible drowning by casting their bait into the churning water from precarious perches on the slippery rocks.

Kane shook his head. "Some people don't have the common sense of a bait fish. Then they expect the rest of us to pick them up and put them back on their feet again, as if they weren't responsible for their own actions."

Margo had the distinct feeling Kane was talking about something that went well beyond the fishermen who had so thoughtlessly put themselves in jeopardy. Intuitively, she knew these strangers were men Kane would feel duty-bound to save if they fell into the water. How she knew that she couldn't say, particularly in light of the warnings she'd been given, and the way he'd blown up the electrical circuits at the mortuary. She simply knew it was true.

Leaning back against a low guardrail, she crossed her arms. "Are you ready to tell me what's going on?" she asked.

Without taking his gaze from the fishermen, he said, "You heard me mention my brother? Alby was four years younger than me and made a career out of being a pest. He thought he was some kind of clown." Kane shrugged. "Maybe that's the only way he could get attention. I don't know anymore."

He lifted one foot and planted it on the guardrail, resting his forearms against his thigh as he looked into the distance. The breeze off the water fluttered his dark hair and spray caught in fine drops between the strands. His bright T-shirt tugged across the breadth of his shoulders, reminding Margo of the strength of his body. And how that same strength could be dangerous to the unwary.

"Since I was the oldest, I was supposed to watch him," Kane continued. "Both of my folks worked. Dad was a machinist and Mom worked at Garrett as an assembler. They worked hard, but we sure as hell weren't rich. My job was to look after Alby."

"Something went wrong." It wasn't really a question. Margo sensed there wasn't going to be a happy ending to this story.

"One day after school he was being particularly obnoxious. Had me running in circles trying to keep track of him. He'd just turned ten the week before and I was fourteen, a freshman in high school. I had a ton of homework to do, I remember that."

He glanced up at the cloud-streaked sky to follow the lazy flight of a pelican before he continued speaking. "The mortuary had been abandoned for years by then. It had always been off-limits. It was like having a haunted house in the neighborhood, I suppose. The kids all stayed away. Except Alby got some kind of a bug up his rear that afternoon.

"I tracked him down there by finding a window he'd broken. It was a dumb kid stunt. Like he thought nobody would notice. He was just hanging around, exploring, and this side of tossing him over my shoulder, I couldn't make him leave. So I told him to screw it. And then—''

He visibly shuddered, and Margo wanted nothing more than to take Kane in her arms. But she didn't dare interrupt the flow of his story.

"Alby didn't show up for dinner and the folks were frantic. I couldn't believe the little jerk would still be at the mortuary... and I... It took me a while before I told 'em what had happened." His hands folded into tight fists and the veins on his arms stood out. "Eventually, they found him in the mortuary basement. Dead."

"Oh, my God..." She ached to let Kane know she understood his pain. He was racked with guilt. She could hear it in his tone and see the remorse in the way he held himself. "It wasn't your fault. You were only a child."

"Yeah. Sure. Except when you're in charge and something goes wrong, you get blamed." His finely sculpted lips canted into a mirthless half smile. "Just ask old Mrs. Cornelius who was at fault. Or my folks, for that matter."

"Surely your parents couldn't have—"

"No? They were in grief, Margo. They tried not to show it, but I could see the accusation in their eyes. They needed a scapegoat. I was handy. After a while..."

"But you were their son, too."

"No. Not really. I was adopted. Alby came along as an unexpected bonus. Their only *real* son."

"Oh, Kane..." If only she had the right to hold him, to ease the furrows that pleated his forehead. He was strong and solid and enduring. Anyone could see that. No family should have punished a child for something that wasn't his fault. She hurt for Kane, for the youngster he had once been, and all of the pain he'd experienced. But she didn't dare act on her feelings. A macho guy like Kane wouldn't easily accept sympathy.

And the truth was, she had misjudged people before. Her husband, for example. A wise woman would make it a point not to leap to any hasty conclusions, and keep her distance.

"There's something else you ought to know before someone else tells you. Like Mrs. Cornelius."

Margo was afraid to ask.

"My biological father was a murderer. He killed two people in a liquor store holdup," Kane told her in a taut voice. "I never knew him. He died in the gas chamber."

The stunning force of shock silenced Margo for an instant. How could a person possibly react to that kind of a statement? Sorrow seemed inadequate, and she didn't know how to comfort Kane.

"How on earth can you be sure of that?" she asked. "In adoptions, the new parents aren't told—"

"Mine were. I was two when my mother relinquished me, fed up with trying to raise me on her own, I suppose. Apparently, the social worker thought I might be genetically predisposed to becoming a murderer and my parents had a right to know. And trust me, my folks reminded me often enough that they'd adopted me anyway—in spite of how I might turn out."

"Did other people—besides Mrs. Cornelius, I mean—know about your father?"

"Most of the neighborhood, I'd guess, and a good half of the kids I went to school with. My parents were particularly proud of having accepted a needy child into the family."

"That must have been terrible for you."

"I got into more than my share of fights as a kid, until I realized if I didn't keep my fists to myself, I might actually hurt someone." He shoved away from the guardrail. "Come on. Let's walk."

Thoroughly shaken, she fell into step beside him. She sensed he needed a break from the emotional memories he'd just relived. She needed a minute to gather her thoughts, too. Little wonder he acted so tough, that he seemed so tautly in control. He'd been fighting his ancestry for years.

Be careful! He might kill you.

The warm wind off the ocean whipped around her and made Margo shiver.

With small-craft warnings in force, most of the boats were tied up at their slips in the marina, their sails furled and their booms wrapped in heavy blue canvas, their cabins draped in the same protective fabric. Sea gulls vied loudly for dominance of the highest masts, resting easily once they won a suitably lofty perch. The boats rocked in the swells. Sea salt and rotting fish mixed in a tangy scent on the warm ocean breeze.

Walking slowly, with a thousand questions still unanswered, Kane and Margo made their way to the busy thoroughfare. Kane stopped beside a street vendor.

"You hungry?" he asked.

"A little." Margo really hadn't given her stomach much thought, not with Kane's revelations about his brother and biological father on her mind. *KILLER,* she realized, had been the younger boy's cruel taunt carved where Kane would be forced to see the word the last thing before he went to sleep and upon waking each morning. If it had been Margo, she would have burned the damn slat. Kane must be a far stronger person than she could ever hope to be.

Or perhaps, she thought perversely, in some convoluted way, he *liked* being reminded of his father's crime. *And* telling others. That possibility sent a renewed frisson of apprehension through her insides.

He bought them both corn dogs slathered in bright yellow mustard. Margo bit into hers and relished a whole raft of memories along with the taste. Carnival hucksters hawking their games. "Knock over the bottles and win a prize. Step right up. Everybody's a winner." And her father holding her up so she could see over the top of the counter.

In spite of everything that had happened, she smiled at the recollection. "I don't think I've had a corn dog since I was a kid going to the county fair with my folks in Iowa."

Kane raised a questioning eyebrow. "You're a country girl?"

"I was. Corn-fed through and through. But my ex-husband, Royce..." The happy memories faded as though washed away by a storm-driven wave. "He didn't like me to talk about that."

"I figured you were divorced."

"Why did you assume I'd been married? Is there some sort of stamp on my forehead?"

"You're too attractive not to have been through the marriage mill at least once. How long have you been divorced?"

"Six years now." She schooled her features not to reveal her surprise—and pleasure—that he found her attractive.

"A lot of marriages crash," he said grimly, indicating little interest in pursuing the subject.

That was all right with Margo. She didn't want to talk about the details of her marriage and divorce, either. Some things were simply too painful to reveal. Besides, she figured Kane was trying to tell her he wasn't the marrying kind. That was fine with her, too. At this point in her life, she was far too interested in getting her own act together to handle a man in her life. After she had left Royce, she hadn't expected things to take one bad turn after the other, draining her limited resources and leaving her in desperate straits.

As they resumed walking, a couple of kids on roller skates sped by them on the sidewalk and bikers maneuvered through the pedestrians in spots where the bike path was too crowded. Bikini-clad girls appeared determined to display all they could to the passing parade without getting arrested. Margo envied their figures, even if their youth made her terribly aware of lost years. Here and there, a homeless person pushed a grocery cart filled with his or her limited possessions and the recyclable gleanings from beach garbage cans.

"Look, Kane," she said as they walked along. "About the mortuary. I understand the death of your brother was a traumatic event, a tragedy of the worst kind, but that doesn't explain—"

"There's more to the story."

Her throat constricted in fearful anticipation. She should have known there would be no simple ending to his tale. "I'm listening."

"About three years after Alby died, two vagrants were found dead in the building. By the time they were discovered, their bodies had turned nearly to leather."

"Leather?"

"It was like they had been mummified."

The corn dog in Margo's stomach turned to stone. "That's weird."

"Yeah." He paused on the sidewalk and impaled her with his silvery eyes. "Particularly since Alby had died the same way. Someone, or something, had drained every last ounce of his bodily fluids."

CHAPTER FOUR

A chill sped down Margo's spine, and darkness, like a lowering window shade, threatened at the back of her eyes. She wavered.

Kane caught her by the shoulders, helped her to sit on a low block wall, and firmly shoved her head down between her legs. She wasn't prone to fainting. Margo knew that. Apparently, the race of blood away from her head had other ideas. While nausea rocked her, she kept her eyes tightly closed.

"Breathe deeply," Kane ordered.

She tried. "I'll be okay in a minute."

"No rush. We've got all afternoon."

And then what? she wondered hysterically. Back to a dark mortuary to make a macabre offering of blood and assorted other bodily fluids to some unknown monster? Human or otherwise? Not exactly what she'd planned for her Saturday evening recreational activity.

Cautiously, she raised her head. To her relief, the earth stayed on its assigned axis.

"You're not joking?"

He shook his head. He was definitely not the kind of guy who made lighthearted jests about life-and-death matters.

"What did the police say about..." She couldn't quite form the question.

"They had a couple of theories, that maybe something occult was involved, or a serial killer was on the loose who liked playing at being a mortician." He lifted his shoulders into a shrug that radiated tension rather than lack of knowledge. Grim lines bracketed his lips. "They had some other ideas, too."

The contents of her stomach did another flip-flop. "What did you think?"

For a heartbeat, he hesitated, then said, "I've never been sure."

Margo's brain whirled with the obscenity of Kane's tale and at the same time denied the possibility that she could be involved in anything so bizarre. Still, she'd heard other rumors, unsubstantiated stories of a very contemporary nature.

"All of that happened a long time ago, Kane. What makes you think history will repeat itself after all these years?" she asked cautiously.

"With the city taking over the mortuary as part of its redevelopment project, and now with the shelter coming in, I think we need to know for sure the place is safe. Particularly after what you experienced last night. Don't you agree?" Kneeling in front of her, Kane deliberately skimmed his thumb alongside her mouth, right at the corner of her lips. For a moment, the sound of the sea breeze roared in her ears, drowning out the pounding of her heart. His touch became heavier, more sensual, and Margo wondered if she would ever be able to breathe again. Or if she would even want to.

"You had a streak of mustard," he said. His voice was lower, huskier than it had been, and rasped across Margo's nerve endings.

She shuddered, although it was impossible to tell if the cause was their morbid conversation, or a jolt of pure unadulterated lust from the intimacy of his touch.

"You were thinking about my safety when you blew the fuses?" she asked, ignoring her accelerated heartbeat that suggested she was already in serious jeopardy of making a fool of herself.

He nodded. "I don't want you staying there alone at night."

"You could have saved the city some money if you'd just told me."

"Would you have believed me?"

"No," she admitted with a shake of her head. "Probably not." The whole idea was too incredible. And yet, this morning, he'd believed *her* bizarre tale. Evidently with good reason.

"Kane, there were stories . . . when the powers that be decided to turn the mortuary into a shelter. People said they found a body . . ."

Kane cursed. Standing suddenly, he speared his fingers through his midnight-dark hair. "When? When did they find the body?"

"In the last few months, I guess. I wasn't paying much attention."

"Dammit, it's happening again, only this time they're keeping it a deep dark secret so the fool city can get the federal funds for the redevelopment project. No questions. No investigation. The city fathers put pressure on the chief to hush up the case before the media got wind of the story. I never even heard any rumors about it so they must have kept it from me, too."

"We don't know that, Kane."

"I do." He paced away from her on the sidewalk, then whirled. "Who was it? Who died?"

"All I heard were rumors." And frankly, she'd been too interested in establishing a homeless shelter for women and children to ask any questions that might prove embarrassing. A seriously shortsighted view, she now realized. "Whoever it was, they buried him at Green Hills as a John Doe. Or at least, that's what I heard."

A pair of passing pedestrians eyed Kane with obvious unease, and skirted around him, glancing just as curiously at Margo.

She stood and closed the gap to Kane. There was no need to discuss gruesome subjects at the top of their lungs for the whole world to hear.

His outrage at the city seemed to have fueled his already pent-up energy. A muscle ticked at his jaw. His fingers flexed in a high-strung struggle for calm and his eyes glinted with the angry blue spark of steel struck against flint.

"Let's walk," Margo suggested. It seemed a reasonable way to help Kane dissipate his tightly coiled tension. Maybe her anxieties would ease, too.

They left the sidewalk to follow the bike and walking path down onto the beach. Sand blown across the concrete, or tracked there by a hundred beach goers, gritted beneath Margo's sandals. The humid air carried invisible crystals of sea salt that teased at taste buds and lodged at the back of her throat. White-capped waves tossed themselves toward the beach with a furious hiss.

Above the wide stretch of sand, a veritable blizzard of Frisbees and assorted beach balls crisscrossed through the air.

They walked a few minutes in silence before Margo said, "After all your bad experiences here in Torrance, why do you stay? Why didn't you simply leave and start over somewhere else?"

"I did leave. As soon as I graduated from high school, I joined the marines. I served sixteen years, all of it running away from my past. A couple of years ago, I realized I couldn't get on with my life until I took care of unfinished business here at home."

"Like finding out who or what killed your brother?"

"That's the general idea."

She shuddered at the thought of the internal demons Kane must have been fighting all that time. "But giving up the marines after sixteen years... You'd almost made it to retirement."

"I'm still in the reserves. You know, weekends once a month plus a couple of weeks at camp every year. Sometimes there are special security projects I'm asked to help out on."

"Security?"

His gaze slid her direction. "Spook projects. Mostly at Camp Pendelton down the coast. Classified stuff."

"Oh." A refugee from the aerospace industry, Margo understood something about security. "Where I used to work I had a Secret clearance."

"But in this case, no need to know," he said, a half smile softening his abrupt halt to her questions.

Because the path was narrow, and the traffic in bikes and people heavy, they had to walk close together. So close their arms brushed from time to time, making Margo acutely aware of Kane's body heat, his size, his sheer masculinity. It figured he'd been a marine. That's what tough, strong, *dangerous* men did with their lives. Or they became cops. Or both. Paradoxically, at some very primal level, Kane both frightened Margo and made her feel safe. Her confusion amplified her reactions to everything he did.

In contrast to the skimpily clad men on the beach, Kane was wearing jeans and scuffed boots. Margo found herself wondering what his legs looked like, if they were roughened by the same dark hair she'd seen on his chest. And how he would fill out a pair of bikini briefs.

Forcefully, she put her questions aside. Just then, the breeze caught a strand of her hair and tugged it across her face. She twisted it back behind her ear.

"So what will you do when you find all the answers you're looking for?" she asked, edging even closer to him as a pair of bicyclists used up too much of their side of the path. "Settle down for good here in Torrance?"

"I don't know. Coming here may have been a mistake. I haven't found answers as to how Alby died—or maybe I've been afraid to look too hard. Recently, a friend offered me a job in Flagstaff. He's got a high-tech security business there. The northern part of Arizona is growing pretty fast."

"I've heard it's nice country." But a full day's drive from where Margo would be working, not just across the street where she might catch a glimpse of Kane as he came and went from home.

He stopped on the path and turned to her. "I think we ought to head back. I want you to have plenty of time to get what you need from the mortuary before it gets dark."

"I really wish you hadn't blown the electrical fuses."

"You may thank me later."

From behind them a voice shouted, "Hey, man! You're blocking the road!"

Margo whirled in time to see a biker barreling down on them at top speed, with his buddy racing along right behind him trying to pass. She froze, unsure of which direction to jump in order to get out of their path.

Kane was quicker.

His arm snaked around her waist. He lifted Margo off her feet and hauled her unceremoniously onto the sand, out of the way of the oncoming bikes. His strength clamped her hard up against his body. Air escaped her lungs in a whoosh even as her fingers curled into his cotton shirt. Her breasts pressed against his chest, her pelvis against his groin. At the swell of her hips, his broad hand branded his heat through her shorts.

As though it were all part of the same motion, Kane lowered his head and kissed her. Hard. And deep. He simply took her mouth with his as if it were the most natural act in the world. And it was.

As natural as the sea grinding away at the beach. As basic as the wind scouring the cliffs.

Margo had dated a couple of times since her divorce. Vaguely, she even remembered kissing a man good-night. But the experience had been nothing like this. Nothing that had made her crave for something more, something that was even hotter and harder, something that fed a hunger so deep, she hadn't known it existed within her.

She wasn't that kind of woman. Her husband had explained all of that in excruciating, humiliating detail. She couldn't have gotten enough passion together to warm up a man who'd been stranded on a desert island for years. She'd been a failure in bed, a failure as a wife.

Yet now, some primitive creature had come alive inside Margo and wanted what Kane Rainer had to offer. Wanted it badly, like the tide wanted to reclaim the shore.

Suddenly, Kane lifted his head, breaking the kiss with a hoarse curse. His eyes were darker now, not like a silvery sky, but closer to the dark regions of the sea— a dangerous place where a woman could drown.

"I shouldn't have let that happen," he said. His hands at her shoulders, he steadied her at arm's length as though he didn't want to have her touching him again.

The primitive door that had opened inside Margo slammed shut. She fought not to flinch at the pain. "No harm done."

"Kids don't have any business racing on the bike path."

"No." Nor did she have the right to dream of things that couldn't be.

He slid his palm to the sensitive column of her neck, stroking her with fingers strong enough to squeeze the life from her body. Or skilled enough to make her body come alive in ways she hadn't imagined possible.

"Dammit, Margo, you didn't even ask me if I killed my brother and all those other people."

Her stomach did another of those lurches that happen when you eat corn dogs and ride the roller coaster one too many times. "Did you?"

His eyes went bleak, as desolate as a landscape ravaged by a plague of locusts. "I honestly don't know."

"What are you saying?"

"I went after my brother that day. I yelled at him, I remember that. And then…the next thing I know, I'm doing my algebra homework, Alby's not there and my folks are asking questions I can't answer. Or didn't want to."

"But the vagrants? If they died in the same way—"

"I'd been out the night before their bodies were found. Just walking. At least that's what I remembered at the time. Later, I couldn't be sure."

"But you're a policeman. Surely the department wouldn't have hired you if there was any question about you being a murderer."

"Maybe I'm an expert at passing polygraph tests."

Margo's breathing was uncomfortably shallow, her throat tight. "But this latest victim. You know whether or not you had anything to do with his death."

"They found the body since I moved back into my folks' house," he told her. "Maybe I have blackouts. Who knows?"

"But you couldn't kill." The words were out of her mouth before she could stop them. Or question if they were only wishful thinking.

She stared at him, the harsh angles of his face. Once again she was acutely aware of the latent power Kane held on such a fine edge.

"I've been trained to kill, Margo. That's what we do in the marines. And I took to the training as though I'd inherited the talent."

His father's terrible legacy. "But you haven't actually—"

"In the Gulf War. It wasn't that hard to do."

She fought to keep the blood from racing from her head to her toes again. "I think you'd know if you were a killer. People don't forget that sort of thing." God, she hoped she was right. *Be careful! He'll kill you.*

"I think we'd better get back to town," he said.

That seemed like the wisest thing to do. She'd be smarter still if she quit hanging around with Kane Rainer.

As they drove back to downtown Torrance, the afternoon clouds that had built up around the mountains were visible in the distance, threatening another night of thunderstorms across the Los Angeles basin. Margo wished the tropical storm would move inland and leave them in peace; she wished she hadn't learned about the hungry place deep inside her psyche. And she wished to goodness Kane had simply assured her he was innocent—that *KILLER* was a prank, not an accurate prediction of fact.

Kane pulled up to the curb in front of the mortuary. "Looks like you've got company," he said.

A bag lady was sitting on the tile front steps. In spite of the heat, she was wearing a heavy black coat and what looked to be several layers of sweaters. Margo knew that homeless people did that for very good reasons. The two shopping bags propped beside the old woman could be too easily snatched from her hands and she'd be left with only the clothes on her back. For women—those of any age—layers of clothing provided an added, sometimes illusional, protection against rape.

It took lots of smarts to survive on the streets.

Margo got out of the car and approached the woman.

"Hello, I'm Margo Stafford. Is there something I can do to help you?"

The bag lady rose awkwardly. She was heavy, and not very tall. Her legs were wrapped as though she suffered from varicose veins, which was entirely possible. Bag ladies spent a lot of time on their feet.

"Name's Penelope Fairweather," she said with an obvious touch of pride. Her gray hair lay flat against her head in a greasy cap. "Heard this here place was a homeless shelter."

"It will be, but we're not open yet. I could call down to San Pedro to see if their shelter has any beds available."

"Nope. Don't bother. I stayed there a night or two, and somebody ripped off my goods." She hefted a shopping bag in each hand. "How soon you figure till you open?"

Margo sensed Kane coming up behind her, but she didn't turn around.

"We're remodeling," Margo told her. "It may be three or four months before we open."

A flicker of surprise crossed Penelope's face. "That's funny. Coulda swore my voices told me to come here."

"Voices?" Margo asked. Like the one that had screeched a warning, not an invitation, in her own ears earlier in the day?

"Sure. It's them voices I hear in my head that make folks say I'm crazy."

Margo nodded. She'd worked enough with the homeless to take Penelope's announcement in stride. It was only her own hallucinations that proved troubling.

"My voices ain't usually wrong." Her smile must have once been stunning but now revealed one missing tooth. She laughed a low cackling sound that somehow invited others to join in the joke. "Maybe I'm crazy, after all."

Maybe she wasn't the only one. "If you can wait a few minutes, I'm sure I can find a bed for you in a shelter somewhere." Margo turned to Kane. "I can use your phone, can't I?"

"Sure," he said under his breath. "But I think you ought to call the county hospital psychiatric ward, not a shelter."

Margo sent him a scathing look.

"It don't make no never mind, honey. It's a nice, warm day. I'll still be 'round when they open up the shelter." Penelope began shuffling off down the sidewalk, chuckling softly to herself. "Less'n my voices send me off on another wild-goose chase."

With a sigh, Margo watched the bag lady trudge down the street. For the moment there wasn't much she could do to help Penelope Fairweather. Maybe later...

"She's nuttier than a fruitcake," Kane said. "She ought to be in an institution, not out on the streets."

"She's probably schizophrenic, and possibly suffering from dementia, but that doesn't mean she's a danger to herself or anyone else. If we could get her on some medication, she might function pretty well."

"Hell, most homeless people are on drugs or are chronic drunks. Your charity is wasted on them."

Margo's eyes narrowed and she fought the rage that made her want to explode. How could anyone be so judgmental?

"I was homeless, Kane." Lifting her chin, she bit off each word with an angry torque of her jaw. "For six months, I lived in my car. No house. No apartment. No roof over my head. Everything I owned was stuffed into the trunk of my car, or in the back seat. I've never in my life taken anything stronger than a pain pill. I don't drink, except for an occasional glass of wine, or a beer. And I am *not* crazy!" She'd been foolish, yes. Unprepared to survive in the real world. But she'd never been crazy...until now. Though there had been moments when she'd wished she had been. Surely her plummet to the depths of despair would have been easier to manage if she'd been a little crazy—unable to recognize how much she had lost.

He stared at her incredulously. "I thought you were one of those rich bitches who drive Cadillacs and live up on the hill."

"I was, before I fell on what one might describe as hard times." Divorce, unemployment and poverty certainly fit into that category. "Though I don't particularly care for your graphic description."

With a still-disbelieving shake of his head, he said, "I'm sorry. I didn't know."

"No reason you should have." It wasn't something Margo intended to advertise. "But just don't ever, *ever* lump all homeless people together. They're individuals with problems, some of which, I hope to God, I'll be able to help them resolve.''

Margo's adamant words rocked Kane back on his mental heels. He'd been so sure Margo was out of his class. That was one of the reasons he'd broken off their kiss at the beach—that and the fact he knew he shouldn't get involved with any woman. He was a man who carried more baggage around than any bag lady could handle. Now he silently reassessed his opinion of Margo Stafford.

She was a survivor.

He still didn't want to get involved. It wouldn't be doing Margo any favors. But maybe, just maybe, they could become friends.

That thought brought him up short. Friendship was definitely not what he wanted from Margo, but in spite of her eager response to their kiss, he didn't think she'd be willing to give more. And a guy who didn't know whether or not he was guilty of fratricide didn't have the right to ask.

Margo turned and hurried up the front steps of the mortuary. She didn't want to be dependent, however temporarily, on Kane for a roof over her head. But after his revelations that afternoon, she wasn't eager to stay in a building that already gave her the creeps. And she was too protective of her limited funds to waste money on a motel room.

Weighing her options, she decided to stay at the mortuary. She'd tough it out. She wouldn't think about things that glow in the dark, or imaginary voices. Nor would she recall the feel of Kane's lips on hers, or the fact that he had such a low opinion of those who were homeless. Certainly, in that regard, he held the majority view.

And she wouldn't think about Kane as a possible killer. She'd simply do the job she was paid to do. Open a shelter.

She slid the key into the lock and opened the door.

The sour, cloying smell of rotting vegetation assailed her, so potent it stung her eyes and drove her back a step.

"Whew!" She turned her head away.

"What's wrong?" Kane asked.

"I've got to get some ventilation in this place. It's like every funeral bouquet ever delivered is still inside the building moldering away. God, it stinks."

Kane brushed past her. "Let me."

She followed him into the vestibule. The stifling heat of the day hung heavily in the high-ceilinged room. She caught the overpowering scent of aged gardenias and wilted chrysanthemums as she glanced up the curved staircase past the stained-glass window. Without direct sunlight, the decorative panel looked dark. Forbidding.

Kiss a killer! Kiss a killer and your lips turn to prunes!

Where the hell had that juvenile taunt come from? The words had simply popped uninvited into her head.

In spite of the heat, goose bumps rose on Margo's flesh. It was only her imagination, she told herself—not schizophrenic voices in her head. Kane's bizarre story about an unknown creature with an appetite for bodily fluids had left her unsettled. That's all.

Still, she was going to stay here tonight. A smart woman simply doesn't move in with a man who thinks he might be a killer. She'd get candles. Or maybe some camping lanterns. Anything to keep the dark shadows at bay.

Kane checked the rooms on the first floor. Apparently deciding there was no immediate danger, he returned to the vestibule and said, "Don't forget the shoes you left by the door."

"Right." Disgusted at the memory, she bent down to pick up the high-heel shoe Mrs. Cornelius's dog had urinated on. When she held it in her hand, the leather cracked and all but dissolved into dust. An uncontrollable tremor began low in Margo's body. "Kane?"

"What's wrong?"

"My shoe. It's..." Fear trembled through her as she looked up into his strange silvery eyes. "My shoe is ruined."

Scowling, he took the damaged shoe from her hand and studied it as though the cracking, dusty leather had committed some foul deed.

"Mrs. Cornelius's dog has a bladder infection," Margo said, amazed at how the tautness in her throat had raised her voice a quarter octave. "Maybe his urine is acidic now and that's the reason—"

"You don't believe that, do you?"

She wanted to. God, how she wanted to. But over the years, she'd learned to be a realist, although in this situation she wasn't entirely sure what reality might be. "Whatever killed your brother is still here, isn't it?"

His strong fingers closed around the shoe. "Get your things," he ordered. "I'm getting you out of here."

CHAPTER FIVE

She shouldn't be here, not in Kane's kitchen. But the reality of her crumbling shoe had been so shocking, Margo had been unable to voice an objection when he'd hustled her out of the mortuary.

"I kinda live on cereal and canned goods here at home, and I eat out when I'm on the job," Kane said. "Hope chili is okay with you for dinner." He scooped the contents of a can into a saucepan.

"Anything's fine. I'm not particularly hungry." Spooky experiences did little for Margo's appetite. She wasn't entirely sure she'd managed yet to digest the afternoon's corn dog, given all the emotional peaks and valleys she'd experienced. Chili wasn't likely to sit much better. "Tomorrow I'll go to the grocery store and see if I can fill up your pantry." If she didn't need her job so badly, she would get on a bus and head for Des Moines, or points even farther east.

"You don't have to do that. You're my guest."

"I've got a real thing about not being dependent, particularly on a man. I've got some money. I'd rather pay my way."

He shot her a curious look from across the room, then his lips curved into a half smile. "I've got a barbecue. If you're interested in buying steaks, I'll cook."

"You don't ask for much, do you, Rainer?"

He shrugged. "I can appreciate an independent woman. Even better if she's wealthy."

"Chicken's better for you than steak. And cheaper."

"Sure. And we used to eat macaroni and cheese when I was a kid because money was tight, but that doesn't mean I wouldn't rather have had a steak."

"Okay, you win." With a nervous laugh, she settled herself in a vinyl-covered chair at the kitchen table. "Tomorrow we'll have steaks. Small ones. I'm on a budget." She hadn't bantered with a man in a very long time. She felt rusty, terribly out of practice, and wondered if she'd chosen the wrong man to spar with.

Did killers laugh and joke like everyone else? Or if you said something to offend them, did they fly into a violent rage?

Kane, she realized, wasn't a man who often smiled. She wished he would. At least that would be reassuring.

He stirred the chili on the stove, then went to the refrigerator. He brought two beers to the table. "How'd it happen?" he asked.

"What?"

"That you ended up living in your car."

She fingered the dampness that had formed on the outside of the bottle. "Like most people, I suppose. Poor planning converged with lousy luck."

He went back to the stove and stirred the chili some more. "You don't have to tell me if you don't want to."

"It's no big secret." At least, most of her past she didn't mind revealing. "I married young. It took me a good many years, but I finally realized my husband was a dominating man who didn't want me to breathe without his say-so. When I tried to spread my wings a little, we ended up divorced. I managed to get a job in the aerospace industry, but you know what happened when peace overtook the world." She laughed without a great deal of humor. "A whole bunch of us landed in the unemployment line."

"California took a pretty big hit after the cold war ended," he conceded.

She unscrewed the bottle cap, idly recalling it had been almost as long since she'd had a beer as it had been since she'd made love. The first sip of cool liquid slid down her throat with a tart bite.

Intelligent women did not contemplate making love with men who might be murderers.

"Then, right after my medical insurance ran out," she continued, forcing the irrational thought from her mind, "my luck went with it. I fell stepping off a curb, and not very gracefully. I broke my ankle." She shuddered at all the painful memories that raced through her mind. Hospitalization. Raging fevers from infection. The searing torture of rehabilitation. "A couple of surgeries later, I was virtually penniless and living in my car." She'd lost not only her veneer of wealth, but that which had been far more precious to her. And completely irreplaceable.

She fought back the tears that threatened. No one, not male or female, could ever understand the pain that still echoed through her soul. The blame was hers. The greatest failure a woman could ever experience.

Kane placed a bowl of chili smothered in onions and cheese in front of her. Steam rose from the dish.

"I'm sorry I mouthed off earlier about the homeless," he said. "But wasn't there someone who could help you? Friends?"

"You use up your friends real fast when you're so needy."

"No family back in Iowa?"

She dipped her spoon into the bowl of chili. "My husband drove a wedge between me and my family almost as soon as we said 'I do.' Clearly—at least in retrospect it became obvious—he wanted me to be totally dependent on him for everything." She lifted her gaze to meet Kane's silvery blue eyes across the table. "Trust me, I'll never let that sort of thing happen to me again."

Kane believed her. He even respected her determination. But somewhere down deep, he regretted Margo didn't want his protection. Given the circumstances, he had little else to offer.

Although even that might be illusory.

Lukewarm water sluiced over Margo in the shower, sending a tiny swirl of fine-grained sand down the drain. Her skin felt particularly sensitive. From an afternoon in the sun, she imagined, or from the arousing remnants of Kane's kiss that had brought all of her nerve endings so close to the surface.

Maybe it was the beer, she told herself, knowing full well her light-headedness at dinner had little to do with alcohol.

She didn't want to think of Kane as a prospective lover, yet that's just what she was doing as she visualized his long tapered fingers stroking her flesh as freely as the warm water spilled over her. He wouldn't appreciate her errant thoughts. After all, he had said the kiss shouldn't have happened. Margo quite agreed. No need to conjure up fantasies about a man set on moving out of state.

A man who might have killed his brother.

Back in the guest room, she picked up her cotton nightgown and started to pull it over her head. Thunder rumbled in the far distance. Closer at hand, a bit a shrubbery scraped against the bedroom window with shivery fingers.

The T-shirt that she'd borrowed from Kane the evening before was draped over the chest of drawers

where she'd left it that morning. She ran her fingertips across the soft fabric. It still carried the winter-
green scent of his detergent now mixing with her own
fragrance.

God, she'd never felt so muddled. So needy. So
frightened that a man she was attracted to might be a
serial killer. She'd seen the frustration in his eyes of
not knowing. His own self-doubt. That feeling echoed inside her chest like a drumroll.

Slowly, she set her nightgown aside and put on his
shirt, the material slipping intimately over her breasts.
Her nipples peaked. She ought to be running for her
life. Instead, she stood in an unfamiliar bedroom,
half-scared out of her wits, relishing the feel of Kane's
T-shirt against her naked skin.

She made it a point to turn off the light before she
got into bed. No way did she want to stare at the word
KILLER inscribed above her head. If the top bunk
hadn't been used for storage she would have slept
there.

As she closed her eyes, her mind wandered with the
ebb and flow of a mental tide, and she imagined the
upper bunk lowering slowly down on her, like the lid
closing on a casket, the satin lining inching closer and
closer until the lid clicked into place.

The panic of claustrophobia gripped her and she
fought the rapid little breaths that threatened her with
hyperventilation.

A blue-green mist rose around her, filling the box with a sickening scent, waving and swaying and flicking moistly across her flesh like subterranean tentacles. Random filaments, as slender as threads of green silk, dragged across her face and slid over her breasts in an obscenely erotic caress.

A scream rose in her throat. Her hands balled into fists and she pounded on the inside of the casket lid.

I'm not dead!

A sound brought her awake with a start. A knocking. Her eyes flew open. On the slat above her, the inscription *KILLER* screamed as loudly as her own cry for help still rang in her head.

Still groggy with sleep, aware only of the gray light of dawn, Margo rolled out of bed and staggered from the bedroom. She fought the lingering effects of the gruesome nightmare.

Kane had already answered the impatient knock at the front door.

"You have to help me!" Mrs. Cornelius's shrill hysteria cut through the early-morning silence like a drill boring through stone. "My little Poopsie. She's gone!"

Kane cupped his neighbor's elbow, ushering her inside as if she were a troubled child. "Calm down, Mrs. Cornelius, and tell me what happened."

"My dog. She went off last night, just ran right out of the yard when I took her out to do her business. Someone had left the gate open. I called and I called, but she didn't come home. I stayed up all night," she wailed. "I didn't get a wink of sleep, not a wink, I've been so worried."

He glanced in Margo's direction. "Why don't you fix Mrs. Cornelius a cup a coffee while I get some clothes on."

"You're a police officer," Mrs. Cornelius complained. She peered over the top of her glasses in an accusing glare. "You've got to help me. It's your job."

"I will, Mrs. Cornelius," he said patiently, "but I don't think my bosses would like the idea of me running around the neighborhood in my skivvies. If you'll just sit here—" he edged her toward the couch "—it won't take me a minute to get dressed."

Her eyes widened as she belatedly realized Margo was in the room, her T-shirt top very much a match for Kane's revealing briefs. Mrs. Cornelius's narrow lips formed a moue of disapproval.

"What you two do on your own time is no concern of mine," she muttered. "I'm simply interested in getting my dog back." She waved a dismissive hand in the general direction of the back bedrooms.

Blazing heat scorched Margo's cheeks. "I'll get dressed and help you look for the dog."

She whirled, but before she reached her bedroom door, Kane caught up with her.

"You don't have anything to be embarrassed about," he insisted.

"I know." Only a wayward thought or two. And nightmares about death and dying that had oddly uncomfortable sexual overtones.

"Even if we had done something..." He ran the tip of his finger down her flaming cheek. "It's none of the old witch's business. We're both over the legal age." His gaze locked with hers, and Margo suspected he could see every one of those wayward thoughts reflected in her eyes.

She swallowed hard. "We'd better get dressed."

"I doubt there's a reason to hurry. If Poopsie had been able to go home, she would have."

"You think she's dead?"

He raised his eyebrows and tilted his head in a noncommittal shrug. "Sometimes animals go off alone to die. And sometimes animals get hit by cars."

"But you're worried there's more to this than simply an old, sick dog who crawled under a bush and couldn't get up again."

"Yeah. I've got a really bad feeling."

Kane's search of the neighborhood was perfunctory at best. Somewhere in his gut he had the awful feeling he'd left a door or window open at the mortuary when he'd checked out the place yesterday.

And because of his carelessness, a poor decrepit old dog had died.

Or maybe, just maybe, he hadn't slept as soundly as he'd thought.

Kane swore under his breath. God, why couldn't he remember what had happened at that damn mortuary twenty-five years ago?

"My dog wouldn't have gone this far away from home," Mrs. Cornelius complained as they circled to the back of the stucco building. "Someone would have had to *lure* her away. Someone not very nice. There are such things as dognappers, you know, and my little Poopsie is a valuable animal."

"I don't think anyone stole your dog," Margo insisted.

At the back door, Kane found what he'd been looking for. The door, with its peeling white paint and half-rotted wood around the lock, stood ajar. He shoved it all the way open.

Can't catch me! Neener-neener! Can't catch meee.

Margo followed Kane into the mortuary. This entrance led to a private mourning room off the big chapel. She could almost hear the narrow hallway throbbing with the memory of a thousand sobbing family members, their tear-reddened eyes accusing Kane of hideous crimes. *Just like his father. A murderer.*

She swallowed back a sob of her own. The voice in her head sounded so real, so close, as though there was someone in the mortuary determined to mock the memory of those who had mourned here. Determined to hurt Kane.

Kane has a girlfriend. Kissy-kissy girlfriend.

Gasping at the innuendo in the taunting voice, Margo grabbed Kane by the arm. "Did you hear that?"

He looked down at her with those icy blue eyes, so pale and detached. "Hear what?"

"Someone—" No, that wasn't possible. Her imagination was simply working overtime again. "I thought I heard something... in the basement." The sound had snaked up through the heating ducts; it hadn't been inside her head. It couldn't have been. Whatever Margo was hearing was a cruel, sadistic presence that seemed to take delight in frightening her. It scraped against her reason with a sinister touch.

"Did you hear Poopsie?" Mrs. Cornelius shoved past them into the chapel. At this early hour, the room was a somber gray with ghostly markings on the dirty carpet to show where pews had once rested. The indentations, like ugly scars, marched to the back of the room. "Where are you, sweet'ums? Mommy's coming."

"Kane, you've got to stop her," Margo said.

"What are you waiting for, young man?" Mrs. Cornelius asked, stepping out ahead of them. "Show me how to get down to the basement. That's where we'll find my Poopsie. I know we will. Such a naughty, naughty girl to have run away like that."

They were halfway across the room when the door slammed shut behind them.

Immediately, the thick smell of wilted flowers rose from the old carpeting, acrid and sour.

"Kane?" Margo asked, her voice cracking on the word.

"The wind."

He was lying. Bald-faced, without so much as a blink of an eye. Mornings were a still time of the day in Torrance. Never a breath of wind until ten o'clock, when the eucalyptus leaves started to sigh against one another in the highest branches, and the coastal fog slipped back out to sea. Then there would be enough wind to lift a curtain, or slam a door. But not now.

They weren't alone.

She whirled to look behind her. But there was no one there. No source of the uneasy raising of hairs on the back of her neck, no excuse for feeling they were being watched.

Icy tendrils, like the seaweed of her dreams, wrapped themselves around her sanity. And squeezed.

Kane snapped on a big flashlight when he opened the basement door.

As Margo followed him into the darkness, the stark white column of light picked up the dangling threads of dusty green cobwebs, then pitched down the steep stairs. It slid across the cracked floor, riding eerily over mounds of dirt and debris. The basement felt dank, she realized, like a swamp formed by rotting vegetation. The moisture clung to her skin and she tasted the decay with every breath she drew.

"Here, Poopsie, honey. Come to Mommy." The older woman's voice quavered, bouncing against mildewed walls with an anxious tremor. "I won't be mad. I promise, sweet'ums."

The moment the light swept over a heap that looked like a dusty ball of fur, fiendish laughter filled Margo's head with sick delight.

Her stomach threatened rebellion and her hand flew to her mouth. "Oh, God..."

Mrs. Cornelius whimpered a pitiful sound that made Margo's chest ache.

"Baby?"

Helplessly, Margo stood by while Mrs. Cornelius crooned a grief-stricken song to her dog and cradled the animal in her arms. The sobs rose in intensity as the woman rocked back and forth.

"Who did this to you, Poopsie? Who did this awful thing to you?"

"Mrs. Cornelius, she was an old dog," Kane said kindly. "Dr. Wiengold warned you—"

"No! Someone killed her. Can't you see that?" She struggled to her feet, her furry burden still in her arms. "Or maybe you don't want to admit that because *you're* the culprit. Oh, I know you. I remember—"

"Mrs. Cornelius—"

"I want the police called. Right now. Right this very minute. And I want Dr. Wiengold to come over here and examine my poor baby. You'll see. You can't get away with this, Kane Rainer. Not like you did when you were a boy."

Kane went as rigid as though he'd been struck by a whip, and Margo was just as shocked by the woman's vicious verbal attack. Even in grief, no one had a right to be that cruel.

"You don't know what you're saying, Mrs. Cornelius." Margo tried to wrap a sympathetic arm around the older woman's shoulders. "You're upset."

Shaking her head, Mrs. Cornelius shrugged away, still holding the bundle of fur in her arms. "Oh, yes, I know what I'm talking about, young lady. I warned you. As the tree grows, so grows the seed. Now look what's happened."

Grim-faced, Kane handed the flashlight to Margo. "See if you can get her upstairs," he said under his breath. "I'll go call headquarters."

"You don't have to do that. The police don't want to have to investigate the death of an old dog."

He raised his eyebrows. "You forget. Mrs. Cornelius has political aspirations. The mayor wouldn't want to give her any ammunition about an incompetent police department that could be used against her in the next election."

Margo supposed Kane was right, but she hated the idea of reopening old wounds. And that's what Mrs. Cornelius had done by accusing Kane of killing her dog.

In contrast, Margo had leaped immediately and instinctively to his defense, she realized. But she'd known him for less than forty-eight hours...

The police officer tipped his cap to the back of his head. He was a burly guy with a face cratered years ago by adolescent acne.

"Seems to me, when weird things happen here at the mortuary, you're always around, Rainer."

"I was at home last night. Sleeping."

"That so? You got anybody who can prove it?"

"No."

Margo stepped forward. "I can. I was at Kane's house all night."

The police officer slid his gaze in her direction, letting his eyes rove in a slow, suggestive perusal. "Looks like your taste in women has finally improved, Rainer. You dated some real dogs in high school."

"Knock it off, Louie, and keep your thoughts out of the gutter. For your information, Ms. Stafford is *not* my alibi. I don't have one. She slept in the guest bedroom and has no idea whether or not I left the house last night."

"So you're still having trouble scoring, eh?"

"And you're still the neighborhood bully, except now you've got a badge that suddenly makes it okay to harass people." Kane made a disgusted sound and turned his back on his fellow officer. Their longtime animosity was so thick, Margo thought it would have taken a chain saw to cut it. How odd the two men would end up on the same police force.

But as she studied the rigid set of Kane's shoulders, she realized what he'd told the officer was true. Though he might have been trying to protect her reputation, she really didn't know how he had spent the night. She worried the thought like a jagged hangnail. It was so hard to believe Kane, or anyone, would creep out of a house in the middle of the night to kill an ancient dog.

She shuddered, unwilling to even consider the dog had died of anything but natural causes.

"What was all that about?" she asked Kane when the other officer walked away.

"Louie is still mad at me because I stole his girl in high school."

"She obviously was the one with good taste."

A little smile twitched the corners of Kane's lips. "Thanks. You didn't have to tell him you'd spent the night. He's so thickheaded, he won't believe we weren't sleeping together."

"That's his problem, not mine." She wished they had been sleeping together. That way, she would have known for sure where he'd been all night and wouldn't be suffering from niggling doubts. "Besides, I thought policemen were all part of the same fraternity. Why would he want to accuse you of killing Poopsie?"

"Let's just say if the rank and file had had any say in things, I would never have gotten on the force in this town."

His words surprised Margo, but perhaps they shouldn't have. If it were widely known that his biological father had been a convicted murderer, it would have made a certain amount of twisted sense that law enforcement personnel wouldn't welcome Kane with open arms. She suspected that his military background had made it impossible for the city, with its stringent civil-service rules, to turn down his application. And there might be a few objective officials in the town who would resist blaming Kane for his father's sins.

Whatever had happened, the atmosphere on the job had to be a living hell for him.

Mrs. Cornelius was still huddled with the veterinarian at the side of the porch. He seemed to be examining Poopsie while at the same time muttering soothing sounds for the pet owner's benefit.

As though Dr. Wiengold had reached some conclusion, he lifted his head and focused his attention on Kane. His mouth drew down with censure.

He approached from across the porch with slow, determined strides. There was hate in his eyes, so much hostility, it was like a slap across Kane's face.

"How did you do it?" the doctor asked.

"Do what?"

"That poor innocent dog. How could you kill one of God's little creatures by drawing every smidgen of blood and fluid from her tiny body?"

A sense of dark menace pressed against Margo's skull. Like the searing flash of a recurring migraine, she knew she was going to hear that taunting, haunting voice again—jeering words about *killing* and *murder*. She took a deep breath. Expanding her lungs slowly, she forced her shoulder muscles to relax, her neck muscles to ease. But it didn't do any good.

KILLER! KILLER! Kane's a killer!

How could he stand knowing that's what everyone thought?

The breeze arrived right on schedule, though it did little to ease the rising temperature of hot, humid air that had hung around the Los Angeles basin for almost a week, and had driven the police back into their air-conditioned patrol cars. Mrs. Cornelius and the veterinarian had left with them.

Standing on the mortuary porch, Margo hugged her elbows to her belly. What the hell was she supposed to do now? She didn't want to go into the building. Not alone. Not where that taunting voice could sneak into her skull once more.

But how could she possibly go home with Kane?

How could he possibly live with all of the cruel remarks that had followed him since boyhood? Whatever had happened to "innocent until proven guilty"?

A black Cadillac that was about ten years from being new pulled up to the curb. The mayor climbed out from behind the wheel.

A tall woman, Marian Westcott walked tilted at the waist as though she couldn't wait to get wherever she was going. She'd been on city council for eight years before she'd run for mayor, and had served on various influential city commissions before that, a virtual fixture in city government. Now she ruled with a steel glove, the single most powerful person in town.

"Hello, Margo," she said with the familiarity that comes with authority. She flicked a look in Kane's direction. "Officer Rainer, isn't it?"

"Yes, Your Honor."

"The chief informed me of this morning's rather unpleasant situation. My guess is that by tomorrow's edition, the death of Bernice's dog will be the subject of an article in the local press. With a good many questions being asked."

"The dog was very old," Kane said.

Mayor Westcott ignored his response, shifting her attention back to Margo. "It's important we avoid any unnecessary controversy about the shelter, Margo. The chamber of commerce is fully behind getting the homeless off the streets. I'm told they inhibit business. And the feds are very disturbed we've been using money to build up the downtown area without providing the required low-income housing, as per the grant contract."

"I understand that," Margo said.

"Good. Then you'll understand why I want us to move with some speed on this project. I want this shelter opened as soon as possible."

"Of course. The workmen will be here tomorrow."

"I want the shelter open within the next ten days."

Margo blanched. "There's a great deal of remodeling to be done first. We have to upgrade the kitchen, put up partitions for privacy in the—"

"You can open before all the work is completed. Order food from a catering service, if need be, until the kitchen is finished. Rent beds, if you have to. And house fewer people than the full cadre, but let's get this place open and running."

"Your Honor," Kane objected, "the building doesn't even have electricity at the moment. There isn't any hot water."

"The city manager has assured me those matters will be taken care of starting first thing tomorrow. Highest priority."

"Still, you can't expect Margo to—"

"I can and I do. If she doesn't think she can manage the project, it seems to me there were any number of applicants for the job. I'm sure we can find someone qualified to take over."

"I'll manage," Margo said stubbornly.

Simultaneously, Kane warned, "The building may not be safe."

The mayor sent Kane a quelling look. "Simply because an aging dog died in the basement of an old building does not imply there is anything inherently dangerous here. If it is Margo's personal safety you're worried about, I'm quite sure you, Officer Rainer, along with the other fine members of our police force, will be able to handle the situation."

There wasn't any point in arguing, Margo realized. In this city, the mayor always got her way. Certainly the homeless never got a vote. And if Margo refused to do the mayor's bidding, she'd be back pounding the streets looking for a job in the time it took for Her Honor to make a single phone call.

As soon as the mayor got back in her car, Kane said, "Why did you give in so easily? You know there's something going on in the mortuary. You've felt it and so have I. It isn't safe."

"I can't simply walk away from my job, Kane. I need the money."

His eyes took on that steely quality that was both hard and unforgiving. "Let me tell you something about my brother."

"Alby?"

"Yeah. He had a mean streak that not many people saw. He'd slick back his hair, tuck in his shirt and smile pretty for his teachers. Our folks. Anybody who came along. They thought he was a damn angel. Naturally, I was the villain if anything went wrong. The bad seed."

"It was cruel of Mrs. Cornelius to say—"

"Alby was the cruel one. Once he caught a stray cat. He lured him into an old wire cage with a few bits of meat and then, until he got bored, he tormented the animal with a sharp stick. Then he set the cat on fire."

"Oh, God..." Margo tried to block the image that blossomed in her mind—a depraved child torturing an animal, laughing with that same fiendish laugh she'd heard in the mortuary. "That happened more than twenty years ago, Kane. Your brother's been dead that long."

"You don't see any connection between the cat and what happened to Poopsie?"

"There can't be." At least there couldn't have been in the world Margo used to know.

CHAPTER SIX

"How can you possibly believe your *brother* had anything to do with Poopsie's death?"

Kane watched Margo pace the narrow width of his living room. She had great legs, a terrific derriere. All of which were shown off to great advantage in the tight pair of jeans she wore. Nice. Very nice. And he shouldn't be thinking about any of that. Not about a woman who was half-scared to death of him. Not about any woman.

"That mortuary spooked you from the beginning, didn't it?" he insisted.

"It's all in my head. Only my imagination."

"The hell, you say." He was across the room in two strides, forcing her back against the wall. Trapping her. Wishing he could feel her lithe body pressed against his. Wanting to kiss her and rip off her clothes, bury himself where she was warm and tight, and knowing he couldn't do that. "That first night we met, you felt something. You were scared spitless. Are you now telling me it was all your imagination?"

She looked up at him with eyes darkened by fear to a deep green. Or maybe what he saw was arousal caused by his blatant sexual aggression. It was hard to tell which. But not hard to know which he wanted it to be, even if he couldn't act on his urges.

"I'm telling you I need to keep my job." Her voice was a little breathless.

"Not at the risk of your own life."

"I don't believe in ghosts. There has to be some other explanation."

"Like me? Do you think I killed that stupid dog?"

The silence roared in the room as if it were a living creature. Accusing. Denouncing the bad seed for what he really was and sucking the last grains of Kane's self-respect from his body. God, he didn't want Margo to believe he could kill anyone, even if it was true.

"No." She said the word so softly, Kane wasn't entirely sure she'd spoken at all. "No, I don't believe you killed the dog."

"Why not?"

She shook her head. "I don't know. But I felt something when we were in the mortuary, and whatever is in that place is evil. Completely corrupt. I don't feel that when I'm with you."

A weight lifted from Kane's shoulders, so heavy he'd hardly realized what a great burden he'd been carrying until he felt it ease.

"You can't be sure," he argued, as much to convince himself as Margo.

She gave him a wry smile. "I don't have a real good record when it comes to judging men, I admit. But then, I haven't had all that many opportunities, either."

Reaching up, he fiddled with the tips of her hair where it skimmed the curve of her jaw. "Your hair's real soft. Almost like silk."

A spark of sexual interest flared briefly in her eyes, and then was instantly doused by her unanswered questions. Kane could hardly blame her. No one would be comfortable in the situation she'd found herself—hanging around with a man accused of the worst kind of atrocities.

"Why don't we try to think this thing through logically," she suggested, visibly backpeddling from too much intimacy. "Who would have wanted to kill a dog, some vagrants, and...your brother?"

"I've tried to puzzle it out. A hundred times. I can't find any connection."

She slid away from him and walked to the far side of the room, but her gaze never left his. And he could still smell the trace of her light scent in his nostrils. Subtly provocative. Definitely tempting.

"Well, then," she continued, "who would know how to..." She closed her eyes as though blocking out the thought.

"You mean, know how to neatly remove bodily fluids from some poor sucker?"

"Yes." The word trembled on a sigh. When she opened her eyes, there was a spark of excitement in them. "The veterinarian! He'd know what—"

"Ol' Walt? He's always been a bit odd, but why would he kill a dog? Much less my brother. And I can't imagine him slinking around spewing out something that looks like a green mist."

"We could sneak into his office after he's gone for the day and look around. Maybe there's a clue. After all, his clinic is right next to the mortuary."

"Breaking and entering isn't one of those things a cop should be caught doing." Although, if Kane thought it would do any good, he wouldn't be averse to trying. He simply didn't think Walt had anything to do with the deaths at the mortuary. "Besides, his clinic didn't open there until after the redevelopment project started. He couldn't have had anything to do with Alby's death."

Her shoulders sagged in a delicate gesture of defeat. "I suppose you're right."

"I've got to go to work in a few minutes," he said, taking a half step toward her, then quickly realizing it was better if they kept their distance. "I want you to promise you won't go over to the mortuary on your own."

"That's an easy promise to make. Not even the mayor can force me to work on Sunday. Besides, word is, she hates paying double time."

In spite of himself, Kane's lips lifted in a faint smile. He was getting too close to Margo. He was beginning to care too much. In the past, he'd never allowed himself to feel much of anything toward a woman. It didn't pay. In time, they always found out about his background. It scared the hell out of them. Somehow, in the face of her very reasonable fears, Margo was still hanging around.

Either she was a very courageous woman...or a very foolish one.

Whatever the case, it made his resolve to get to the bottom of the goings-on at the mortuary all the more urgent.

He waited until his shift was over. Only four cars patrolled Torrance streets on a Sunday night, fewer after midnight. The malls were closed, the bars quiet. Even the career criminals who hit on fast-food hangouts and convenience markets seemed to have taken the night off. Evidently, the crooks had to spend some time at home with their families.

He used Margo's key to let himself into the mortuary. She hadn't realized he'd kept it.

Standing in the foyer, he listened to the night sounds. An occasional car rolled by on the street. A few blocks away, a train rumbled along the tracks, vibrating window casings in the mortuary that had grown loose with age. In Kane's inner ear, he registered a low throbbing sound, the steady cadence of muffled marching troops, that could have been his own pulse beating. Or the rhythmic expansion and contraction of the building as the night air cooled the structure, like the heavy breathing of something supernatural.

He'd been here before. Listening. Trying to penetrate the secrets of the past. But never before while the force had been so active. The killing force.

When his eyes adjusted to the dim light slanting through the stained-glass window from the street, he sat down on the curving stairs that led upstairs. Drab unsightly patterns of olive green and splashes of dried blood-red dappled the carpeting in odd contours, meaningless shapes made somehow more threatening by the very fact of their being muted and ill defined.

Holding a heavy metal flashlight in his hands, Kane waited. And remembered.

Sweat trickled down his temple and edged past his jaw to creep down his neck. Distant thunder from another sweep of a tropical storm echoed a warning in the mountains that surrounded the L.A. basin. And still he didn't move.

The streets grew even less well traveled—no headlights flashed across the stained glass to give it life or artistic form; the hum of freeway traffic five miles away vanished into oppressive silence.

In the darkest part of the night, at that hour well past midnight when death stalks the unwary, he caught the scent of putrid vegetation. It swirled around him like the fog of decay. Ugly. Tainted by cruelty. Conjuring grotesque images of a young boy's face floating bodiless on a sea of slime. Smugly taunting at first, then contorted with terror.

Neener-neener! Can't catch meee!

Kane listened, immobilized by the voice that sliced like sharp razor blades through his brain. The visceral pain deadened his awareness. The jeering words whipped across his psyche at a deeper level, one that built his rage to a white-hot fury. He tasted the bitterness of the past like bile that won't stay down.

Killer! Killer! Your daddy's a killer!

"Dammit, Alby! I'm going to kill you if you don't come outta there!"

Stupid pickle-brain, I'll tell Mom if you do. She loves me best!

Kane leaped to his feet, his pulse surging painfully through his body. His uniform shirt was soaked through with sweat; his body trembled with anger. And shook with fear of the truth.

Around his legs swam a blue-green mist, looking like the gaseous tentacle of some hideous creature, distorting images, playing an evil game with his mind, teasing cruelly at his knees. It weaved in and out, sliding past his trousers, searching—Kane sensed on some instinctive level—for food. It scuttled low around his feet.

The mist moved and writhed with the hypnotic power of a trained cobra. A fascinating dance with death. Dulling to the senses. Paralyzing.

Kane became aware that both of his ankles burned as though they'd been wrapped in an acid bath. But a strange lethargy drained him of both the energy and will to withdraw. He was like a long-distance swimmer who had reached the limits of his endurance and was willing to slip under the waves to find peace.

His body tensed and he fought the sensation. "No! Leave me alone, Alby."

But I wanna play.

"I won't let you—" Moving abruptly, he broke the hypnotic connection. His muscles trembled with the effort he'd exerted.

He switched on the flashlight, beating at the insubstantial mass with the heavy weapon. Something sparked, the flashlight batteries fusing in a wisp of smoke before the column of light went dark. The metal case of the flashlight scorched his palm. The mist retreated, shuddering for an instant before it attacked again.

Kane took advantage of that minuscule lapse in the mist's burning grip, and ran for the door.

At the sound of squealing tires in the driveway, Margo was on her feet and racing for the back door. She hadn't been asleep. Instead, she'd been watching the minutes tick by, waiting for Kane to get home, worrying when he was late and growing more and more frantic as the hours crept toward dawn with still no sign of him. She hadn't fretted that much about anyone in a good many years. And knew she didn't have the right to question Kane's whereabouts now.

But she'd been so damn scared. Irrationally so.

She yanked open the door.

With wooden movements, and a face that was ashen, Kane tossed his big metal flashlight onto the kitchen counter. It landed with a crash, pivoting in a half circle before coming to a rolling stop. The silver casing was scored by a wide, irregular band of black.

"What...what happened?" Margo asked.

"I learned that whatever is going on at the mortuary, it has nothing to do with Walter Wiengold."

"You went back there? Alone? After you warned me off?" A combination of panic and concern raised her voice several decibels. "Are you crazy?"

"Possibly." He unbuckled his gun belt and put his weapon in the drawer by the door. His hands trembled and Margo knew something truly frightening must have happened to unsettle him so.

She forced herself to stay calm. Kane was safe, no harm done. "You want a beer?"

"Yeah." He sat down at the kitchen table and, elbows propped, dropped his head to his hands. Sweat stained his shirt under his arms.

Margo twisted the cap from the beer and placed it in front of him. She waited until he stirred himself enough to take a long swallow.

"You want to tell me about it?"

"The thing...whatever it is...attacked me."

"Attacked?" She choked. Kane had said the word with deadly calm, as though it were an everyday occurrence for something to creep up out of the bowels of a mortuary basement to assault an innocent passerby. "How? Why?"

"Why? It may not seem very rational, but I had the sense it was...hungry."

Margo felt the color drain from her face. Some unknown creature *feeding* on bodily fluids? The unearthly thought sent a roil of terror through her stomach and a wave of dizziness swept over her. "Were you hurt?" she said a moment later.

He hiked up a pants leg. "There. On my ankle."

"Oh, my God..." Angry red blisters circled his ankle. She knelt and tugged down his sock. "It's like a burn."

"Hurt like hell, on both legs, but it's okay now. Hardly stings anymore."

"You need to put some ointment on that." Standing, she ordered, "Get your pants off. I'll find something in the medicine cabinet for that burn."

"I'm not going to take my pants off in front of you," he sputtered.

"Don't go modest on me now, Kane. I've already seen you in your underwear. And so has Mrs. Cornelius," she reminded him. "I promise I won't ravish you any more than she would."

As soon as Margo returned to the kitchen with some ointment, she questioned the wisdom of her promise.

Kane's legs were well muscled, lean and sinewy, roughened by dark hair that swirled up his calves and across his thighs. Swallowing hard, she knelt at his feet. It took her a moment before she could tamp down the surge of need that suddenly overtook her, a wanting so fierce she reeled at the impact. It wasn't like her to react so intensely to a man, any man. But then, admittedly Kane was more virile than most she had met.

She palmed his calf, lifting his foot to inspect his injury, trying not to think how she would like to caress his legs and thighs and every intimate part of him. Somewhere deep inside, she felt an unfamiliar clenching of muscles. Her mouth went dry.

Try as she might to resist it, her body appeared determined to react in a very primal way whenever she was around Kane.

With her fingertips, she applied the lotion, smoothing it across the welts that marred Kane's warm masculine flesh.

"This isn't like any burn I've ever seen," she said, gamely trying to concentrate on her task and not the warmth and texture of Kane's leg. "There are a thousand tiny pinpricks, every one of them blistered."

She shifted her attention from his ankle, up his leg, and halted at the nest of his hips. She gasped. He was fully aroused, big and hard, his engorged organ stretching the cotton fabric of his briefs to the limit.

So big she wondered how any woman could possibly accept...

Her gaze snapped up to meet his silvery eyes, dark now with his arousal. Heat flamed her cheeks.

"I'm sorry, Margo. I looked around for a pillow. Or a napkin..."

"It's all right. I didn't mean to—"

"Your position, sitting there between my legs. It didn't take much imagination to—"

She scooted back. Her imagination had been playing similar tricks on her, creating images of uninhibited lovers freely touching and caressing and kissing in ways she had never truly experienced. Ways she had no right to contemplate with Kane.

She allowed only a very small part of herself to rejoice that at some level he wanted her, too.

"The ointment ought to take the sting out of those burns," she told him. Her legs felt too weak to stand, so she sat there on her knees, on the floor, feeling foolish. And needy. And wishing she were the kind of woman who knew how to please a man.

He hesitated a moment, a muscle working at his jaw, his long fingers curled tightly around his beer, before he said, "I think tomorrow I'll try to get a copy of the autopsy report on that John Doe you told me about. The one they found in the mortuary."

"What will that tell you?"

He shook his head. "I don't know. But maybe if he has burns on his body like those—" Kane indicated his ankles "—then I'll know for sure I didn't have anything to do with his death."

"You still doubt that?" Her eyes widened. How could Kane still think of himself as a killer? Unless, God help her, it was true.

"I have to question everything, Margo. Most especially my own actions. That's how they train us at the police academy."

Kane watched as Margo rose to her feet a little unsteadily. He should have helped her up. But he was in no condition to play the gentleman.

When she told him good-night and left the room, he could finally unclench his teeth, as well as relax certain other blatantly tense parts of his anatomy. The mild sting circling his ankles had been nothing compared to the excruciating pain he'd felt in his groin with Margo kneeling at his feet.

Normally, he had himself under better control.

The blue-green mist slithered around her, searing her most private orifices with intimate strokes of its tentacles. In those tender places where nerves bunched together, it caressed, aroused and menaced all at the same time, striking a sensual chord, then punishing her for responding. Twisting and turning, she tried to escape, but the incessant stroking continued, her writhing making the pain all the more acute. And the pleasure more intense.

Arching against the most private kind of invasion, she could no longer tell where her body ended and the unrelenting tentacles began. The burning torment pulsed within her. She couldn't escape.

She sobbed a low, throaty sound and clenched her fists. Tears dampened her cheeks.

Turning, she pleaded for mercy—or for release— and Kane was there. Towering above her. His strange colorless eyes like two lasers intent on destroying her, or sucking the life from her.

She sat up with a start, cracking her skull on the bunk slat above her. *KILLER!*

"The work order should say four phones," Margo insisted. "One in my office upstairs and three down here on the first floor."

"General Services only signed off on the three downstairs phones, ma'am."

"Just how do they think I'm going to run this place without a phone in my office?"

The telephone installer shrugged his shoulders. "You want me to start with what I've got?"

"Yes, go ahead." She'd have to fight with the pea-brains in General Services later.

Over Kane's strong objections, she'd opened the mortuary this morning in time to meet the workers who were scheduled to arrive. "Nothing bad has happened there during daylight," she'd argued with more conviction than she felt. "And if I don't show up, I'm fired. The mayor made her position quite clear."

Now there were two men ripping up the old carpeting in the chapel area, and a couple more were trying to get the recalcitrant hot-water heater installed. Electricians buzzed around, trying to undo the hash Kane had made of the wiring. Upstairs, carpenters worked at demolishing the old kitchen from the walls out, their hammers resounding through the building. The mayor certainly knew how to get a project moving.

If only the closed door to the basement didn't loom quite so large in her awareness, Margo would be more content with the morning's progress.

Ring around a killer and we'll all fall dead!

Margo shuddered.

"You all right, ma'am?" the telephone man asked, his boyish face troubled.

"Yes, I'm fine." Nothing could hurt her in the middle of the day with a dozen workmen in the building. Even the smell of decay seemed less intense today, as though the presence of so many people had driven the putrid odor out of the building. Or back down into the earth.

As she made her rounds to check on the workers in the chapel, she spotted Penelope Fairweather peering in through the back door. She'd leaned her bags against the doorjamb and seemed to be taking in all the activity.

"I'm afraid we're still not open, Penelope."

"Oh, that's all right, honey. I jes' like to keep track of what's going on in the neighborhood. Heard on the street some poor lady had her dog die in this here building."

"Yes, it was Mrs. Cornelius. Her dog got out of her yard somehow."

"Ain't that a pity. I remember when we used to have dogs. Cats, too. That was before my Eddie passed on. Pets are a real comfort when you're lonely. Cain't quite remember what happened to them sweet little creatures."

"Do you have any children?" Margo thought if she could reconnect Penelope with her family, maybe they'd provide her with a home and proper medical attention.

The older woman looked at Margo through weary, rheumy eyes. "They don't have no more use for me, honey. Cain't say I blames 'em, me being pretty fargone most days."

Margo took her hand. "Won't you let me find you a bed at a shelter? They'd help you find your children—"

"Don't fret so, child. This here ain't such a bad life, not when I got my voices to keep me company."

"I wish I could let you stay here, but it's just not possible." And would be entirely too dangerous until she and Kane could determine the source of the evil that haunted the building. And put a halt to it.

What she could safely do, Margo decided in a flash of insight, was to find a way to connect Penelope with Mrs. Cornelius. The two aging women needed to have someone to care about, and it wouldn't hurt the neighborhood busybody to think of someone besides herself.

But Margo's thoughts were interrupted by the plumber shouting, "Hey, Ms. Stafford, you wanna come check out the water heater?"

"Be right there," she responded. Maybe after she got the shelter safely open and running, there would be time to introduce Penelope and Mrs. Cornelius.

Before Margo could excuse herself, the bag lady said, "You seeing that fella I saw you with yesterday?"

Margo fought a blush that threatened. "He lives in the neighborhood."

"He's got funny eyes. Spooky."

"They're not spooky at all. They're simply... different." Verging on strange, Margo admitted, but a man shouldn't be blamed for the genes that had given him an unusual eye color. *Or a father who was a murderer.*

Penelope laughed that infectious sound that ranged somewhere between insane and having-a-good-time. "If you say so, honey, but he'd be a hard man for me to trust."

"He's also a Torrance police officer."

"See? What'd I tell you? Not a trustworthy man in the bunch." Penelope cackled her laugh one more time, picked up her two bags and shuffled out the door.

Margo wished she could deny she'd had a few second thoughts about Kane, too.

He showed up at the mortuary about three in the afternoon, dressed in his uniform, the very image of authority, ready to take on the bad guys who slipped into town during his shift.

"You going to close up shop pretty soon?" he asked.

"Most of the workmen are gone, but I've still got some paperwork to do. Somebody messed up the work order on the phone installation."

"I want you back over at my place before it gets dark."

For some reason, Margo bristled. Maybe it was because of the odd dreams she'd been having. Or the warnings about Kane she'd received from half the neighborhood, including bag ladies. Or even more likely, it was because she hated to be bossed around after years of kowtowing to her former husband.

"You're hovering, Rainer."

"You're not planning to stay here tonight, are you?"

"No, not if I'm still welcome at your place." Though the choice put her in an uncomfortable position between a rock and a hard place. "It seems the electricians are having some difficulty undoing whatever it was you did to the wiring. It may take them a couple more days to get everything rewired."

"Thank God," he mumbled.

"Kane, this is my job. I'm going to do the very best I can to open this shelter. When I'm done with my work for the day, I'll go home, and not a moment before that." Odd that she'd think of Kane's house as her home, however temporarily. She certainly had no right to claim any part of it as her own.

A movement at the front door attracted her attention.

A man, whom she guessed to be about seventy years old, stood at the entrance looking uneasily around the foyer. From the crisp fit of his shirt and the expensive silk tie he was wearing, Margo instantly calibrated the gentleman was not a candidate for a homeless shelter.

"May I help you?" she asked.

"No, not really." He walked inside, glancing at the stained-glass window, then into the chapel. "I didn't mean to interrupt."

"We're in the midst of remodeling."

"Yes, I read about it in the paper. I used to work here."

"Work?"

"An apprentice mortician. A long time ago. In fact, I started work in '35, the day before the Long Beach earthquake. Not a date easily forgotten." He smiled

benignly, a practiced smile Margo suspected funeral
directors had perfected since the beginning of time. "I
read a dog died here yesterday. Under unusual circumstances."

Margo shot Kane a questioning look.

"It was an old dog," he said.

"I know. I just thought, from the report in the paper..." He walked toward the basement door and
simply stood there staring at it. "There were times
when a body would come in late at night. We'd check
it in, chill it down, then go back to bed, figuring we'd
take care of embalming it in the morning."

The stranger turned. He was a slender man with serious eyes. "It was peculiar, really. I never quite understood it. Sometimes, when I went downstairs the
next morning, there weren't any bodily fluids left to
drain from the corpse."

CHAPTER SEVEN

She waited until the stranger had left, waited until she could get upstairs to her office, away from curious workmen, then Margo turned to Kane, who had followed her. If anything, the chill at the base of her skull was more intense now than it had ever been.

An aberrant force. Here in the mortuary. For sixty years!

Her tremulous smile came from a measure of victory. "You didn't have anything to do with your brother or those other people dying here," she told Kane.

"Didn't I? That man downstairs told us something bizarre happened to bodies that were already dead when they arrived. When Alby broke into the mortuary, he was very much a living, breathing pest. And I still can't remember what happened, or even if I followed him inside."

Margo's confidence plummeted. She'd been so sure the stranger had exonerated Kane of any wrongdoing. Now...

Killer! Killer! Can't kiss a killer! The juvenile taunt threatened to unhinge her. The chill deepened, racing down her spine, burrowing into her and making her shiver from the inside out. She desperately wanted Kane to be entirely guiltless. Wanted a chance to—

Her mind cut off the forbidden thought, even as she struggled to defend his innocence.

"But the... thing... attacked you last night. You can't be responsible..." Tears pooled in her eyes. "Oh, Kane..." Her feelings about him were so jumbled, a topsy-turvy mix of fear and longing, it was little wonder she was confused. Yet she knew instinctively that he had the power to stop the lonely shivers that had racked her life for so many years, if only he would wrap his arms around her.

As though he could read her mind, he did just that. She went into his embrace easily, pressing her head against his broad shoulder, her cheek against the starched fabric of his blue shirt where it covered the hard, unyielding bulk of his bullet-proof vest. Automatically, her arms circled his lean waist. Swallowing a sob, she vowed not to leave tearstains. A man, particularly a cop, wouldn't want to go to work in a shirt thoroughly soaked by a hysterical woman.

"Shh, Margo, I'll promise you one thing. I'll never hurt you. I swear it." His words were husky and rough-edged with emotion as he squeezed her tight.

She clung to his promise like a talisman after he left for work. But the truth was, if Kane was guilty of murdering his brother during some sort of a mental blackout, then he was fully capable of killing again.

* * *

He'd made it to the station just in time for roll call. Then he'd ducked upstairs instead of going out on patrol. One of the good things about being an outcast in a tight group like a police force was that you could go anywhere and people made it a point to ignore you, sometimes not even providing backup when you radioed for help. Even the secretaries had gotten the word about Kane Rainer. They didn't mess with him.

Which made it all the stranger that Margo seemed to be so comfortable in his house—and in his arms.

Under the circumstances, he wasn't sure that was fair to her—or to him. He'd spent a lifetime wanting things he couldn't have no matter how much he fought and clawed for them. Not much had changed over the years.

He weaved his way through the upstairs offices to the records section.

Computerized police reports made it easy to cross-reference almost anything. Sitting at an unoccupied console, he searched through the files for John Does. There weren't many in Torrance. It was the kind of town that claimed their own—all except Kane, who'd never been welcome.

Why don't you go back where you came from, ape nose? Mom and Dad don't want you anymore.

Kane commanded the screen to scroll through the John Doe case dated only six months ago. When he got to the autopsy report, he stopped.

"Rainer, aren't you supposed to be out on patrol?"

He typed a print-file command before he responded to the lieutenant's question. Somewhere in an adjacent room he knew the printer's acknowledgment light had begun to blink.

"I had something I wanted to check," Kane said. He killed the screen with another few strokes on the keys.

"Yeah, well...be careful out there tonight. There've been some gang rumblings in the L.A. strip. Their grief might ooze onto our turf."

"So I heard." Kane stood. Lieutenant Ramsey was all right. Though the man was never really cordial, Kane hadn't felt from him the animosity that he'd experienced from others on the force.

"You'll watch your back?"

Kane nodded. "I always do." As he headed for the room that housed an array of printers, Kane had the distinct impression he had just been warned.

Margo hated Monday-night football.

She'd tried a sitcom and found no humor in it at all. For whatever reason, Kane's country-western and soft-rock CDs held no appeal tonight. Maybe she was too aware of being a woman alone to enjoy the heart-tugging sorrows of others. Even meditation hadn't distracted her from thoughts of Kane.

So she listened with one ear to the inane football announcers analyzing a game where the score was so lopsided it was boring, and kept an eye out the front window watching for Kane's patrol car. It was too early for him to come home, but she thought maybe he'd drive by. Just to check.

She could see the mortuary from where she sat curled up at one corner of the couch—the homeless shelter, she mentally corrected in the hope that the name wouldn't conjure up the usual string of macabre images. Except for a single streetlight, the building was a dark silhouette against the orange-tinted night sky. Ominous. Silently threatening.

It's all right. I won't hurt you.

The voice she heard wasn't an echo of Kane's earlier words, but a more childish call like the *ally-ally-oxen-free* cry from her youth. Yet it wasn't coming from inside her head, from her memories.

It was coming from the mortuary.

Muted, distant and somehow plaintive. Like a child who was *it* and couldn't find anyone to tag.

Without any thought, she was on her feet and out on Kane's porch staring at the mortuary looming across the street, the air outside as sweltering as it had been in the house. There wasn't anyone in that dark building. She'd checked every door, every window before she left for the day. No one could get inside. Certainly not a lost little boy.

She hugged herself as she might have hugged a child. She felt so empty. So alone. And the building called to some instinctive urge she'd fought to suppress. Because she had failed so dismally.

Tentatively, she stepped off the porch. The television voices droned behind her. She'd be a fool to go to the mortuary now. In the dark of night. Alone.

Yet she felt irresistibly drawn...

At some level, she became aware of a more urgent voice on the television, a special announcement. The commentator excited.

"...the gang-related shooting in Torrance has left one police officer wounded and a suspect dead. The officer has been taken to Torrance Memorial Medical Center where his condition has not as yet been reported. Officer Rainer is a two-year veteran—"

She didn't stop to lock up the house. She simply got her car keys and left, making it to the hospital in less than five minutes. Once there, she brazened her way into the emergency room, right past a couple of cops drinking coffee from paper cups.

A painful band squeezed the air from her lungs when she spotted Kane. He was propped up in a sitting position on a gurney, his dark evening whiskers in stark contrast to his unnaturally pale complexion. His eyes were closed; his chest moved slowly as each shallow breath tugged at his shapeless hospital gown.

Margo fought the trembling of her chin. How had she so quickly come to care about this man, a man who she also feared might be a murderer?

Hesitantly, she took his hand. His fingers closed around hers and his eyes opened, silver-blue and intense. The corners of his lips slipped into a half smile.

"I didn't expect company."

"I heard about it on TV." She stroked the back of his hand with her thumb, flesh that was strong and very masculine. "They didn't say how badly you were hurt."

"Bruised ribs. The bullet knocked me off my feet, but the vest did its job. Unfortunately, I cracked my head when I fell. The doctor figures I've got a mild concussion."

"Could have been worse, I suppose." He could have been dead, and if that had happened, the pain in Margo's chest might never have eased.

His gaze shifted to the two police officers lounging with studied disinterest across the room. "Yeah, it could have been better, too." He drew a deep breath that caused him to wince. "Let's see if we can get out of this place." Sitting up, he threw his legs over the side of the gurney.

"Kane, you can't just walk out of here. Concussions can be serious. You need to wait until a doctor releases you."

"So find one, or I'll check myself out."

Margo did as he ordered. In a hurry. When she got back to the curtained cubicle, Kane had already pulled on his shirt and was trying to button it, his fingers working with clumsy inefficiency.

"I'll do that," Margo said. And she'd do it without reacting to the jagged hole in his shirt right over his heart. Thank God for bullet-proof vests.

"I'd be happier if you'd stay a while longer, Officer Rainer," the doctor said, arriving in Margo's wake. "But it appears you'll be in good hands with your wife. And probably rest more comfortably at home."

The doctor's assumption of their marital status went unchallenged. Margo figured it was easier than offering explanations about their relationship, a connection that eluded definition even in her own mind. Kane probably felt the same way. Was he simply her host, like an innkeeper? Or were they roommates? Certainly not husband and wife, or even lovers. No, not that . . .

"Mrs. Rainer, I want you to wake him every hour or two," the doctor continued. "If he becomes nauseated, or if his headache becomes too severe, double vision, any of that, I want him back at the hospital. Double quick. And you need to watch his eyes, Mrs. Rainer, for any unusual dilation."

"I'll take good care of him, Doctor."

The man smiled at her a little tiredly. Based on the number of patients visible in various examining areas, Margo guessed it had already been a busy night. The doctor was probably happy to clear out one of the beds.

By the time they got home, it had started to rain, big spattery drops that did little more than muddy the windshield and nothing at all to cool the tropical air temperature. The wipers smeared the mess from side to side without really cleaning the glass.

Margo pulled up at the curb in front of Kane's house. "Where's your patrol car?"

"They probably hauled it back to the maintenance yard. It's kind of missing a windshield now, and there's at least one flat."

The persistent ache in her chest drew tighter. He'd come so very close to death....

"Let's get you to bed."

He popped open the car door. "Best offer I've had all day, *Mrs. Rainer.*"

She ignored his bantering tone and hoped he wouldn't see the quick flush that she felt rise to her cheeks.

As Margo exited the car, she caught a movement across the street, a shadowy figure at the side of the mortuary, too ill defined to be identifiable. At the same time, a blue-green light licked across an upstairs window.

Ally-ally-oxen-free! Can Margo come out to play?

Suddenly disoriented, as dizzy as if she were the one with a concussion, her head ringing, Margo had to steady herself with one hand on the fender. She swallowed hard. Now was not the time to lose her equilibrium. She had to get Kane inside, to bed. Hearing taunting voices in her head was definitely not on her agenda for the rest of the evening's entertainment.

Once in the house, she helped him shrug out of his shirt and loosened his shoelaces. With his toe against his heel, he pushed off the shoes.

Though she'd had glimpses of his bedroom, she hadn't been inside before. The furniture was heavy and a little ponderous. Still, Kane looked too big for the double bed. Only a king-size would allow him to stretch out comfortably, unless he slept corner to corner. Then there would be no room for him to sleep with a woman.

She wondered at the way her mind was working tonight.

"I suppose you want me to take off my pants again?" One corner of his mouth canted into a mock-lecherous grin. She suspected he was reacting to the medication he'd been given, not to her sex appeal.

"And get under the covers," she ordered. "If you think you can manage alone, I'll turn my back."

"I'll manage."

Trying not to picture exactly what was going on, she heard rustling sounds behind her, and the squeak of the bed as he settled down. His pants had been carelessly tossed over a chair. She picked them up, folded them neatly and looked for a hanger in the closet, aware of the lingering heat from his body still warming the tightly woven cloth.

She knew he watched her every movement. Intently. In response, low in her body, his heat seemed to seep into her. Her throat felt parched, the tight band around her chest all the more achy.

"You want to talk about how you got shot?" Margo knew she didn't want to discuss what she was feeling, the unfamiliar urges that were notching up her personal temperature one degree at a time. Kane wouldn't welcome the knowledge.

"I got in the middle of a gang rumble. Two cars full of opposing players. I knew it was going to get messy."

"Didn't you call for help?"

A muscle ticked at his jaw; his lips thinned. "My backup didn't arrive for a full thirty minutes."

"They must have been busy. I mean, you can go the whole length of town in a half hour during rush hour, for heaven's sake. A hell of a lot faster with a siren blaring. What took them so long?"

"They were sending me a message, Margo. Get out of town."

Shock made her reach out to Kane in what was meant as a reassuring gesture—or maybe she simply had to touch him to reassure herself that he was still very much alive. Her hand trembled as she smoothed back a lock of his rumpled hair from his forehead. My God, how could he have come back from the marines to live in a town that didn't want him? A place where neighbors accused him of terrible crimes, and his co-workers put his life in danger to send him the same ugly message?

He caught her by the wrist. "I am going to leave, Margo. As soon as I know that mortuary is safe for you and the homeless you're so worried about, I'm outta here. It's not worth my life to stick around."

"I understand." It made a whole lot of sense for Kane to stop punishing himself by living in a place that held nothing but contempt for him. But, God help her, Margo would miss him.

She slipped her hand from his grip. "You go to sleep now. I'll, ah, check on you in an hour or so." Without meeting his gaze, she switched off the bed lamp, sending the room into near darkness.

"Margo?"

"Yes." She held her breath.

"Thanks for bringing me home."

Emotion filled her throat so completely, she was unable to respond. Kane was going to leave.

After the second time Margo woke Kane to check on his condition, and he rolled over mumbling something about how she should quit bugging him, she settled down on the straight-back chair beside his bed. For comfort's sake, she'd changed into Kane's T-shirt that she'd been using for a nightgown. But she knew if she went to bed, she wouldn't wake for the hourly medical exam, as per the doctor's instructions.

The next hour crawled by with impossible slowness. Her eyelids were so heavy, and the chair so hard, she thought maybe if she lay down next to Kane—on top of the blankets—then his movements would wake her soon enough. After all, she hadn't slept with a man in a good many years, and Kane filled most of the bed. She was bound to grow uncomfortable squeezed so close to the edge.

Kane's room had an oblique view of the street. She hadn't remembered to close the shade and the diffused illumination of a streetlight blurred the outline of the mortuary across the way. The illusion made the building appear to float over a treacherous black chasm of darkness, shadowed in a mysterious haze.

Help me! Help me! It's trying to kill me!

Margo sat up with a start, her pulse leaping. "Kane!" she said.

He rolled over. "What's wrong?" His words slurred with sleepiness.

"At the mortuary... There's a child... Someone's trying to... We've got to help him."

She got out of bed and made for the door, but Kane snagged her before she got to the hall.

"No."

At his uncompromising command, her head snapped up. "What, no? I'm telling you there's a child—"

"It's your imagination. There's no one there."

"But I heard him."

"Think a minute, Margo. A kid could scream his head off over there for days, and you couldn't hear him from this distance. Besides, the building's all locked up, isn't it?"

Her confidence slid away under his intense scrutiny. "I was so sure..."

He took her by the shoulders. "It's the middle of the night," he said gently. "You were probably dreaming."

Yes, that was no doubt the case. One of those demon voices that had been plaguing her had simply entered her dreams. Again. "I'm sorry I woke you."

"No problem." His hand slipped to the column of her neck. Slowly, his thumb measured the length of her jaw.

"You probably ought to get back to bed. The doctor said—"

"I'm feeling much better now. Much better."

She knew she ought to pull away, step back at least a little to put some small amount of distance between them. He wasn't holding her, yet she felt shackled by the strange steely blue of his eyes. And by his heat.

Then, as he dipped his head toward hers, she realized it was too late to escape. Nor did she want to.

At first, his lips were a sweet torment, torturing her gently. Slanting his head, he insistently flayed her lips with kisses that banished all awareness except the electrifying thrill of his mouth on hers. His lips were firm and warm and determined, tasting of the remnants of evening coffee and the seductive flavor of sleep.

Margo gave herself over to the sensation of curling warmth that thrummed low in her body. No other man had ever made her feel this way. So filled with wanting, so thoroughly female. She'd only dreamed, in her most fanciful moments, that she could respond to a man like this.

His tongue slipped easily past her lips and she uttered a throaty sound at his determined invasion.

She arched against him, closing tight the door on a small part of her brain that still feared Kane was a killer. For tonight, she needed what he made her feel, needed to forget past failures and ignore the future.

His fingers splayed through her hair, capturing her head in a tender vise as he plundered her mouth. He stroked the dark recesses he found, creating within her a honeyed brightness that rivaled the sun's. His hand found and cupped her bottom, pressing the center of her need ruthlessly against the hard ridge of his arousal.

Pleasure shot through her.

She twisted into the nest of his hips, wondering whether the torture of wanting was greater for him, or for her.

A groan vibrated from the depths of his chest.

His hand slid under her T-shirt, palming her ribs, moving with excruciating slowness upward—ever upward over her needy flesh. She waited in eager, desperate anticipation for the touch she longed to feel. Her nipples rose to aching peaks.

"Oh, Kane, touch me." She couldn't breathe, she couldn't think.

He swore, low and harsh, his body shaking with sudden tension. "I can't...we can't do this, Margo." He swore a second time. "I'm sorry." His breath came hot and fast as he continued to hold her tight.

It didn't matter.

Her arousal, her excitement, had been doused as effectively as a poorly placed sand castle washed away by a renegade wave. All of her insecurities resurfaced. She'd been told, more than once, that she wasn't capable of pleasing a man. She should have listened. That way, this stark reminder of the truth wouldn't hurt so much.

"You're right." She placed her palms on his chest and pushed herself away. Her legs felt weak, her spirit drained. "You've had a serious injury to your head and you need your rest."

"That's not what I mean, Margo."

"Go back to bed, Kane. I think you're well enough that I won't have to check on you anymore tonight." With her head held high, she fled from the room, hiding the chilling sense of shame, of failure, as she had throughout her entire marriage.

But tonight she couldn't face the demon memories that often came with sleep.

Kane found her the next morning curled on the couch, still awake, staring into a fireplace with ashes as cold as the empty place in her heart.

CHAPTER EIGHT

She looked up at him with eyes she knew damn well were red-rimmed.

"I've been calling myself all kinds of a fool for sending you away last night." His voice was low and early-morning rough. Raspy and so sexy it sent even her deficient libido into orbit. Standing by the doorway, he was barefoot and wearing jeans. An ugly blue bruise darkened the left side of his chest.

"I'm not crying about what happened between us." Old news about her continuing inadequacies shouldn't have the power to bring so much pain. She'd cried those tears years ago. "Royce, my ex, explained to me any number of times that I'm not exactly the sexiest woman around."

"Is that what you thought? That I broke it off because you're not sexy enough?"

"It doesn't matter, Kane. It's something I've learned to live with." She pulled her knees up to her chest and wrapped her arms around them, as if by pulling herself into a tight ball, she could ward off the truth of her deficiencies.

"You're wrong." In two long strides he was across the room. He towered above her. Intimidating. Forceful. Dangerous to her heart as well as potentially dangerous physically. "You are the sexiest woman I've ever known. Just being around you, I get a hard-on that won't quit and hurts like hell."

Unable to meet his gaze, she studied a small ink stain on the sofa cushion in front of her toes. "You don't have to lie."

"Dammit, Margo! Look at me. I'm not lying."

Slowly, she raised her eyes, trailing up his muscular legs encased in denim, and halting with a start at his crotch. The telltale bulge was unmistakable. Thrilling.

But why now? Why, when he hadn't wanted her last night? In spite of an equally determined arousal.

"I don't understand," she whispered.

He knelt, bringing his face close to her. "Half the neighborhood would like to see me run out of town on a rail or maybe strung up. My co-workers are of the same bent. And I don't know whether they're right or not about what I've done. *No* woman needs that kind of grief."

With the back of her hand, she gently rubbed the ugly bruise on his chest. The dark swirling hair was silken, achingly sensuous as the strands curled over her fingers. "You were playing the part of a noble, self-sacrificing hero?"

One side of his mouth lifted into a wry smile. "Not exactly typecasting, is it?"

She paused a moment, weighing the many facets of this dark, dangerous man. "Yes, I think you probably play the role of noble hero more often than you care to let on." But she hadn't expected him to reject her through his own martyrdom.

"Trust me, I'm not usually quite so virtuous as I was last night. Given a second chance, I may not pass the test again."

Breath lodged in Margo's chest. "I'm probably the one who would get a failing grade. I'm not very good at—"

Catching her hand, he said, "Your ex really did a number on you, didn't he?"

"Maybe he was right."

"Honey, if he didn't get satisfaction out of you, when you're so hot, so damn giving, the problem was *his,* not yours."

Her insides clenched as though he had actually stroked them.

She desperately wished Kane were right. But he didn't know the deep, dark little secret that proved beyond all doubt that she lacked some vital element, some missing ingredient that left her less than a whole woman. He deserved to know the truth.

"I really wasn't crying about what happened last night when you came in. I was crying... Today is my son's birthday."

He raised a questioning eyebrow.

She went on with her confession, her voice a little tremulous, her throat aching. "Stephen's sixteen today. He and his brother, Richard, live with their father in Sacramento. Two years ago..." She swallowed so painfully it was like swallowing tacks. "I voluntarily relinquished their custody to Royce." She struggled not to sink into a black sea of shame. How could anyone—man or woman—understand why she'd given up her babies? Her precious babies...

Why do we have to go? Don't you love us anymore, Mom? Oh, yes, my beloved babies. It'll just be for a little while.

Kane looked at her in stunned disbelief. "It doesn't sound to me like there was anything *voluntary* about you giving up those kids. Your love for them is written all over your face. What happened? Did that cretin of an ex-husband take you to court?"

She shook her head. "I called *him*. I'd lost my job, and then broke my ankle. Things were spiraling downhill and I knew I was going to lose the house, too. I was going to be homeless, Kane, and I couldn't bring myself to put the boys through that."

"What about welfare?"

"I was off my feet for so long, I couldn't even properly care for them. I thought it would be best—"

"Has your ex got money? Couldn't he have helped you out?"

"He'd already lived up to his part of the divorce agreement—to the letter, as he often reminded me. He was never once late with his child-support payments, but it wasn't enough. And once he had custody, he didn't have to pay anything."

Kane stood and speared his fingers through his already sleep-rumpled hair. "So he just left you to sink or swim on your own. I'll bet he's damn proud you ended up living in your car."

"He didn't know. No one did." She'd been the one with the pride, so much so that she hadn't wanted anyone to know of her failure.

"What about your kids. Do they know?"

She shook her head. "Richard, in particular, is very sensitive. I didn't want to worry him."

Kane muttered a string of angry expletives under his breath.

"So now you see why the job at the shelter is so important to me, Kane." She shifted around to sit more squarely on the couch. "I'll have a place where they can come visit me. Maybe at Thanksgiving or Christmas. For a few days, anyway. I miss them so much."

"Yeah, I can understand that."

He paced across the room, as though trying to reach a verdict. Margo had never felt so vulnerable, so exposed. She half expected him to ask her to leave. To find her guilty of the worst crime a mother could commit—giving up her children.

Turning, he stared at her. Some small part of her self-esteem that she'd managed to retain through all of her tribulations began to wither. *Guilty as charged.*

"You want to make a call?" he asked.

She frowned. "Call?"

"It seems to me a kid would like to hear from his mother on his birthday."

"I sent him a present. It wasn't much. Just a Dodgers' T-shirt, but he was always a fan."

"He wants to hear your voice, Margo. It's early enough so you can catch him before he goes to school." Kane gestured over his shoulder toward the kitchen and the phone on the wall. "Call him."

Hungrily, Margo's gaze slid in that direction. "I'll pay you for the call."

"Just do it, Margo. Call your kid."

Kane took his time shaving and getting dressed. He wanted to give Margo plenty of space to make her phone call. It seemed to him he hadn't done her much of a favor last night by playing the "noble hero," as she'd called him. He'd hurt her. He'd never meant to do that.

But he hadn't lied to her. He'd wanted Margo Stafford since the moment she'd arrived at his house. He simply didn't think he had much to offer in return.

When he wandered back to the kitchen, she was fussing around the stove.

"Your breakfast is almost ready," she announced with a brightness that surprised Kane. "Hope a cheese omelet is okay. Your larder isn't exactly cordon bleu quality."

"An omelet's fine but you don't have to fix me breakfast."

"Oh, but I like to cook. It's one of the things I do really well. Or at least, I used to."

He studied her hurried, almost hyper, preparations. "How's your son?"

"Terrific. He didn't have too much time to talk, though."

"How come?"

She dropped a couple of pieces of bread in the toaster and pressed down the lever. "His father gave him a car for his birthday. Steve was pretty excited. He wanted to check it out. A TransAm, I think he said. Can you imagine? Sixteen years old and he has his very own new car."

Kane came up behind her and slid his arms around her waist. She felt both fragile and tense with repressed tears. "So how did he like his T-shirt?"

She hiccuped in a way that sounded suspiciously like she was swallowing a sob. "Turns out he's a Giants' fan now. No loyalty at all..."

"Yeah, well, you didn't have any way of knowing that."

"I should have. A mother should know things like that about her son." She twisted in his arms and buried her face against his shoulder. The tears came then, loud and hard. Her slender, delicate body shook with them.

Helpless, all Kane could do was hold her until the sobs eased. He ached in ways he hadn't known possible, for dreams lost—or dreams never quite formed. For intimacies he'd never been invited to share.

"I'm going to lose him, Kane," she finally said, sniffing. "I'm such a rotten mother, I'm going to lose my baby."

"Don't be so sure. Besides, there isn't a mother in the world who could compete with a guy's first car."

She lifted her head. "You think so?"

"I'm absolutely positive." He placed a soft kiss on her forehead.

Making an effort to blink away her tears, she gave him a weak smile. "Thanks. I needed that."

"My pleasure, ma'am."

She punched him lightly on the arm. "And don't call me ma'am. It makes me feel ancient."

"Oh, yeah? Just how old are you?"

"Thirty-six, not that it's any of your business."

"You're right. Absolutely ancient. But you're still young enough to have a half-dozen more kids."

"A half dozen?" she sputtered.

"If you wanted."

"Well, I wouldn't."

"How 'bout one or two? If the right guy came along."

Her hazel eyes widened with incredulity. "I doubt very much that's going to happen."

"You never know." He threaded his fingers through her hair, tucking a few flyaway strands behind her ear. He wasn't quite sure what had started him down this line of conversation, but he knew it was dangerous. Very dangerous.

He cleared his throat. "The toast popped up."

Blinking again, as though she didn't quite understand what he'd said, she broke the spell he hadn't entirely meant to weave. But the thought of Margo having babies—his babies—was one that he couldn't so easily set aside.

Electricians. Plumbers. Carpenters. They had her on the run upstairs and down. But not in the basement. If anyone went there, she didn't know about it. Didn't want to know.

Now that the ugly beige carpeting had been pulled up, revealing equally ancient and stained plywood, the odd, warped areas where heat radiated up through the floor were all the more apparent as she made her rounds. Margo would have to ask the workmen about that phenomenon.

On the good-news side, this morning the odor of wilted flowers appeared to have gone into hiding.

Can't find me! Can't find me!

She shuddered. Whatever taunting voices were haunting her, Margo had no desire whatsoever to find the source.

As she came into the vestibule, she spotted Penelope standing at the open front door peering inside.

"You're keeping close tabs on us," Margo said with a smile.

"Always was one to want to be where the action was."

"Come on in, if you'd like." At the very least, Margo could offer the bag lady a safe spot to rest for a while.

"Not sure as how I ought to do that. Got business to tend to."

"Business?"

She set down her two bags, then delved into one, pulling out a puppy, of all things. He was brown and white and all floppy ears.

"How adorable," Margo said.

"I found Algernon in a Dumpster, I did. Poor little tyke had been thrown away like he wasn't no better'n trash. Figured that there lady who lost her dog recent like could use a new one to love."

"Oh, I don't know. Mrs. Cornelius might not be ready for a replacement just yet."

"Well, I sure cain't keep him, much as I'd like to. Cain't hardly feed myself, much less a dog. And if I turn him over to the pound, sure as shootin' they'll put Algernon to sleep."

That was probably true, although puppies had a better chance of being adopted at the Humane Society than adult dogs did. "I don't know," Margo hedged.

"Reckon it cain't hurt none to ask."

And maybe, Margo mused, a bag lady's act of kindness might soften up Mrs. Cornelius about her new homeless neighbors. It would certainly provide an excuse to get Penelope linked to the neighborhood busybody, and hopefully the connection would develop into a friendship that would benefit both women.

Margo glanced around the foyer. No workmen were waiting for her further instructions. This seemed as good a time as any to sneak out for a few minutes.

With an approving nod of her head, Margo said, "Let's see if Mrs. Cornelius is at home."

The woman's house was across the street from Kane's, an almost matching bungalow with a yard that was neat as a pin. Roses were still in bloom on carefully tended bushes; the lawn was lush and precisely trimmed. A low chain-link fence separated Mrs. Cornelius's fifty-foot-wide lot from her neighbors. The No Solicitors sign on the gate was no doubt meant to discourage strangers.

That certainly seemed the case when Mrs. Cornelius answered the doorbell. She peered through the screen with no pretense of friendliness. "What is it you want, young lady?"

"This is Penelope Fairweather. She heard you'd lost your dog and was kind enough to think of you when she found a puppy in the trash."

On cue, the bag lady produced Algernon for inspection.

"Found him in the trash? Why ever would you think I'd want a dog like that? My Poopsie had very impressive papers, a pure bloodline that went back generations."

Once on his own feet, Algernon's tail starting ticking like an overwound metronome.

"Well, this here little guy weren't so lucky," Penelope said. "When he came down the assembly line, they couldn't even find a pair of ears that fit him. And didn't do much better with his feet."

In spite of herself, Mrs. Cornelius's lips twitched into an amused smile, softening her angular features into a face that was almost beautiful. "I'm sorry. You'll have to take him back. I really can't—"

"Take him back where?" Penelope asked. "To the Dumpster back of the thrift shop where I found him?"

"To the pound, then. I simply don't want—"

"I don't exactly have no car to take him there. Maybe you could do that for me."

Algernon pawed at the screen door and whined.

"I'm far too busy—"

"Tell you what, missus. If you'd just keep little Algernon for an hour or two, I'll ask around. I reckon I can find somebody to take him to the pound, like you said. And he won't be no trouble, not with this nice yard you've got.''

''Well, I don't know...''

''I surely do appreciate your help, missus.'' Ever so politely, Penelope smiled at Mrs. Cornelius. ''And if you do have an old leftover can of dog food, I imagine Algernon would be mighty happy to finish it up for you. Reckon he hasn't eaten in some time. Lord knows, I didn't have no money for buying dog food.''

Margo was in absolute awe of Penelope's ability to manipulate Mrs. Cornelius. There wasn't a crazy bone in the bag lady's body this morning, only cleverness. And maybe a fair share of wisdom. Because, before they headed back for the mortuary, Algernon had already wormed his way into Mrs. Cornelius's reluctant heart.

To Margo's surprise, Kane showed up at her office in late afternoon, dressed in his uniform. Her heart did one of those strange little somersaults that happened whenever he appeared unexpectedly.

''After the shooting yesterday, shouldn't you at least take a day off?'' she asked.

''I don't plan to give them the satisfaction.'' His grim statement reminded Margo that Kane placed the blame as much on his peers as on the gang bangers who had shot him.

She resisted the urge to hug him, to plead with him not to put his life on the line again for people who didn't give a damn. But Kane wasn't a man who listened to that kind of advice. Stubborn and intractable came to mind. Honorable, too.

Handing her a sheaf of papers he'd been carrying, Kane said, "In the excitement last night, I forgot about the autopsy report on the John Doe. It makes for real interesting reading."

She leafed through the pages. A shudder raced through her as she picked up words like *desiccated* and *mummified.* Horrid pictures popped into her mind. Grotesque skeletons covered by skin turned to leather, their mouths twisted into the rictus smiles of the dead, their bodies stacked one on top of the other in the mortuary basement.

Ally-ally-oxen-free. Can Margo come play?

Her hands shook and she folded the papers in half. "I'll read this later, after I finish up some paperwork I have to do." And when she was a little more prepared to deal with the grizzly details of the vagrant's death.

"We can't let the city move any of the homeless in here until we find out how that man really died," he said.

"The mayor stopped by today. She wants me to open the shelter by next week."

"She must have her head in the sand. This place is dangerous." He swore and rubbed his hand along the back of his neck. "I want you back at my place before dark," he warned.

"I will be." She certainly had no desire to hang around the mortuary after dark, and she suspected the autopsy report would be a chilling reminder of the *thing* that had wrapped itself around Kane's ankle.

"Remember, it's getting dark earlier every night. The time change—"

"Are you trying out for the nag-of-the-year award?"

"Not likely. I'm trying to keep you alive."

Renewed anxiety slammed into the pit of her stomach. "You be careful, too."

"Yeah."

He hesitated for a heartbeat, and she thought for a moment he might kiss her. His eyes had darkened, his gaze focused on her lips. Suddenly, she was aware of the bed in the room adjacent to her office, and the primal aura that emanated from Kane. At some very fundamental level, she responded.

Then he whirled abruptly and marched out the door.

Margo squeezed the autopsy report tightly in her trembling hands. She could not let herself think about possibilities. Or temptations. Not when Kane had made it abundantly clear he was leaving town and didn't want to leave behind any unfinished business.

Fighting tears, she turned and stared at the back of the room, at the cupboard door that still remained unopened. She still had no idea where the key might be, or if there even was one.

* * *

The cloying scent of gardenias reached her as she finished the last notations on work-order changes. Like eighth-grade graduation, she recalled, when all the girls had been wearing identical white dresses pinned with corsages provided by the town's only florist, and the auditorium got steamy with the presence of too many bodies.

The scent snagged at the back of her throat.

"Where on earth is that coming from?"

Standing, she stepped out of her office. Though outside it was still daylight, shadows steeped the hallway in deep gloom and funereal quiet filled the building. Even the traffic sounds from the street seemed muted by an eerie grief. Phantom voices whispered in her ears.

I'm scared. Don't leave me here alone.

She walked slowly forward. Listening. Her heart thrust with unnatural force against her ribs. She breathed shallow irregular gulps of air to avoid being overwhelmed by the heavy scent of decaying vegetation, sickeningly sweet.

At the top of the stairs, she stopped. From that angle, gruesome images slashed the stained-glass window like ugly caricatures of waiting corpses. Red and yellow and bilious green.

It's dark. Help me.

She covered her ears with her hands. It did no good.

Don't be mad at me. I didn't do anything wrong.

She tugged her lower lip between her teeth.

Lethargy dragged at her will; time passed in slow motion. The worn wooden banister felt smooth beneath her palm, warmed by a thousand mourning hands. Leading her downward.

In the vestibule, she stopped at the door to the basement. Beyond that portal lay perilously steep stairs and the child who was calling to her. Like one of her own children . . .

Cautiously, Margo reached for the doorknob.

CHAPTER NINE

"Margo! Dammit, Margo, where are you?"

Kane tossed the Chinese takeout on the kitchen counter. He'd figured there wasn't much left in the house for her to eat, so he'd taken an early Code Seven for a dinner break and come back home.

But there was no damn sign of her and the house was dark.

He checked her room. No purse. No indication she'd come and gone.

Where's your girlfriend, Kane? What if I've got your girl?

"Dammit, Alby! Leave her alone."

Kane raced out of the house, stopping only briefly at his patrol car. He had to keep his wits about him. This was not the time to panic. Margo's life might depend on his keeping a cool head.

Adrenaline shot through Kane as he sprinted across the street. The taser gun he'd pulled from the patrol car felt heavy in his hand. And a little crazy. But he knew a bullet wouldn't stop whatever evil thing was in that dark, brooding mortuary.

Mom'll be mad if you hurt me.

"Shut up, Alby."

He reached the double doors to the building. With grim determination, he settled his breathing and ordered his heart to slow to a manageable beat. Fear clamored for his attention. He responded with measured, sweat-filled calm.

He tried the door.

The latch clicked and released. Cautiously, he pushed open the door. It swung back on its hinges with a low groan of complaint. From within the building a rush of putrid air assaulted Kane. The scent of death.

Kane gripped the taser gun more tightly as he edged into the interior shadows.

There, fifteen paces away, the door to the basement stood open. Glowing blue-green.

"Margo..." Her name was a plea on his lips. A prayer from the soul of a man who hadn't prayed in a very long time.

She stood on the top step as though in a trance. Hungry blue-green tentacles licked toward her like the tongues of hell.

Go away! She wants to play with me.

"No!" Kane bellowed.

I'm gonna tell!

"Go ahead."

He poked the taser into the swirling, undulating mist and pulled the trigger. An electric jolt shot into the gaseous mass. One tentacle retreated. Minimally. He gave it another shot.

You're not playing fair.

"Neither are you. You never did."

Kane linked his free arm around Margo's waist. "Come on, baby, let's get out of here."

He nearly lifted her off her feet and headed for the door. She seemed disoriented, still under the spell that had held her captive. She stumbled and Kane caught her up in his arms.

The tentacles surged after them in an angry, roiling river of green. The air became unbearably hot, singed with the stifling scent of rotting vegetation, a gagging press at the back of Kane's throat. His legs grew heavy. He felt as though he were running through waist-deep water dredged up from ancient sewers.

He burst out the front door onto the porch. Painfully, he dragged in a lungful of fresh air, and pulled the door shut behind him. Vaguely, he was aware of the bag lady loitering on the sidewalk. But he didn't stop. He wanted to get Margo safely home.

"I can walk," she protested, her arms linked around his neck.

"Not yet." He wanted to keep on feeling her in his arms. To know she was alive. Unharmed. To never let her go, even though he had no right to claim her as his own. His fear had fueled the inner fire that had been smoldering for days. Only Margo could cool the flames that threatened to engulf him.

He carried her into the house. He got as far as the living room, then lowered her to her feet. His body pulsed with his need. Tension thrummed through his veins like wind through taut wires. He had to have her. He had to reassure himself that she was okay, that she had escaped the demon mist.

"Margo...God, Margo...I need..."

"Yes." She knew exactly what he needed. It was written in the steely blue of his eyes, that deepening of intensity, the sharp edge of desire. And it thrilled her beyond measure, even blocking the memory of terror from her mind, that Kane would want her as surely as she wanted him. With his passion, she could bury a lifetime of nightmares. Together they could reaffirm life, the triumph of the living over the dead, the present over the past.

"If you want me to stop, God help me, I swear I will. Just say the word."

"I want you to love me, Kane. Now."

Almost before she had finished giving him permission, he crushed his mouth against hers. There was nothing gentle about his taking what she had agreed to share. It was needy and primitive. His tongue plundered her mouth. His hands stripped her of clothes, and then he did the same for himself. There was no time for Margo to worry about her inadequacies. Only time to feel, to react to a building whirlwind of desire.

To his carnal maleness, she became a woman at the same elemental level. Free to pleasure, and seek pleasure in return. Uninhibited by fears. Driven by instincts she hadn't known existed within her.

She touched him, kissed him, explored his body with abandon.

They reached the bedroom and tumbled together across the bed, Kane spreading her legs with the press of his thigh. She writhed beneath his weight. Her fingers tested his shoulders, his back, his buttocks, kneading his muscled flesh in a wild effort to bring him closer.

A red haze of pleasure followed wherever his lips traveled, awakening uncounted erogenous zones— along her neck, her breasts and nipples, the dip of her stomach, and finally the place where she desperately needed his touch.

"Kane, oh...please..." She begged for his mercy, for the ultimate release that had always eluded her and now, at last, she felt was within her grasp.

"It's all right, baby. Let it go..."

"I can't..."

He slid into her, hot and hard, so deep he stroked the farthest recesses of her womb. She arched up to him. Helpless. Impaled on a pillar of sweet, hot pleasure.

"Yes, baby. You can do it." With guttural words, he urged her higher, faster, until she was flying, shredding apart. He lifted her hips and drove even deeper into her. She screamed. Her body convulsed around his shaft, once, twice, and then he penetrated beyond all barriers, the involuntary clenching of her muscles spilling his seed into her.

He called her name roughly, the sound like trumpets heralding the victor.

This is how it was meant to be, Margo thought, awed by the power that continued to surge in rippling waves through her body. Then all thought was lost when he moved within her again and she sped into a place of light so pure and glorious that it held no beginning and no end.

Margo suppressed a sigh. She didn't want to leave the cocoon of Kane's embrace. She definitely didn't want to think about the implications of these last few passionate minutes. Nor what had led up to them. She simply wanted to float forever on this sated feeling of contentment.

Shifting his position, Kane untangled his legs from hers and pressed a kiss to her temple. "I've got to go check in with the dispatcher. Don't go away."

Go away? Not likely. She felt so boneless, she could hardly move. But her balloon had certainly sprung a leak and she was coming back down to earth fast. Too fast.

She shuddered and sat up. What the hell had happened to her at the mortuary?

Kane returned to the bedroom before she had satisfactorily answered any of the questions that were beginning to plague her.

"You okay?" He'd gathered her hastily discarded clothes and placed them on the corner of the bed. He hadn't bothered to dress. His magnificent body was still hers to feast her eyes upon. And, Lord help her, she wanted to feel the rough, rugged length of him pressing against her—inside her—again. She doubted she would ever tire of the sweet pleasure of Kane possessing her.

"I'm fine. Terrific."

He gave her a long, lazy perusal that made her skin flush. "I'd be the first one to agree with that verdict."

"I don't usually... I mean, I've never—"

"I know."

Sitting down beside her, Kane finger-combed a few strands of her wayward hair, gently pushing them behind her ear. He was so at ease with himself, so comfortably naked, it allayed some of her embarrassment. And reduced not one iota of her wild need to love him again.

"We're going to have to talk about what happened," he said.

"Just now?"

"We'll talk about what happened between us later. Right now, I need to know what happened in the mortuary. Why didn't you come home when it got dark?"

"I meant to." It took a real effort to shift mental gears from the feel of his fingers, the sight of the swirling dark hair on his chest and the way it arrowed to the nest of his now-flaccid manhood. "I was finishing up some paperwork when..." She raised her eyes. "I'm not sure it will make any sense to you."

"Probably not, but nothing does these days. Give me a try."

"I felt drawn. Downstairs. To the basement."

"How?"

"I heard a voice. I thought...it sounded like my boys calling. One of them needed me."

"No!" Anger flared darkly in Kane's blue eyes. "It wasn't your son. It was Alby. My brother."

"What are you saying?"

"I hear the voice, too, and I know damn well who it is. He's been taunting me since I got back to town. Particularly whenever I go near the mortuary."

Margo's stomach lurched. "You mean, you think that green mist is your brother's ghost?"

"I don't believe in ghosts. Or at least I never have before."

"But we already know there was something...evil about the mortuary before your brother was even born. How could Alby be haunting the place now?"

"I don't know. I only know I don't want you to go back there again. Ever. Not until we're damn sure it— whatever *it* is—is gone."

"You know I can't just quit my job. I need—"

He grabbed her roughly by the shoulders, his fingers—minutes ago so gentle—now pressing hard into her flesh. "What you need is to stay alive. You can live here with me. No strings attached. For as long as you want."

"You're looking for a roommate?" Her foolish imagination had conjured up an entirely different image of the future. A typical female reaction, she realized, and terribly unwise.

"Your kids can visit. Anytime, for as long as they want to hang around. I'll even move out, if that's the only way you'll quit that damn job."

His fury stunned her, and the implications of his words. *Don't worry. I'll take care of you. You aren't smart enough or tough enough to manage on your own.* She tried to ignore the echo from the past, one she'd vowed never to hear again.

"Even if I didn't need the money—which I do—I'm not sure I can simply turn my back on the homeless shelter. If *it,* that force, was responsible for killing Mrs. Cornelius's dog, and that vagrant they found, and now it has managed to lure me to the basement— very likely for the same purpose—what will happen to the people who will eventually move in there? People who are counting on the city to provide them with a safe place to live. We can't just walk away..." She swallowed hard. "They'd die."

"We'll tell the city not to open the shelter."

"I'm not at all sure the mayor would be willing to listen. Her reputation is all wrapped up in the downtown redevelopment project. And unless we can get

that green mist to attack *her,* well, she'd never believe
us."

A corner of his lips twitched into a grim line. "Now
there's an idea. We could lock the woman—"

"Kane!"

"All right. All right. I know this isn't something to
joke about." He linked his hands behind his neck and
rubbed as though trying to rid himself of tension.
"I'm just so damn frustrated by this whole mess. We
don't even know what we're fighting."

She scooted around on the bed until she was kneeling behind him. Placing her hands on his shoulders,
she began to use her thumbs to knead the muscles
across his back. "It seems to me, if there was something going on in the mortuary before the war, then
that force must have been there even earlier than
that."

"Not much was happening in Torrance until about
1913," he said. "That's when the town was founded,
and there wasn't any serious growth until after World
War II.

"And the Miller Mortuary was the first mortuary in
town. It's even been declared a historic building.
They're going to put up a plaque."

"Hmm. So I heard."

She smiled as she felt him relax a little. Kane was a
very intense man. He needed someone to help him
handle stress. Maybe she could teach him meditation.

Over the past few years, it had helped her considerably.

Then she remembered he was planning to move to Arizona, and she'd be living who knew where. It was unlikely there would be many chances for her to teach him anything, or to soothe away even a day's worth of strain.

Valiantly, she pressed the thought to the back of her mind. No sense buying trouble before it shows up. Patience had been one of the lessons she'd learned during her long months of rehabilitation on her ankle.

She bent forward to place a light kiss on his shoulder while she continued her massage. His skin was slightly damp with sweat and tasted of salt. He smelled of virile sex and masculinity, a heady scent she would always remember and yearn for.

"Indians..." His voice caught on a husky note.

"What about them?"

"They were here before the town."

"Oh. Yes. I suppose that's true." But it didn't seem to matter, because she'd become increasingly aware of a reawakening of sexual interest throbbing low in her body. Of course, she wouldn't expect Kane to share her newfound enthusiasm for the act of making love. Though she felt she had satisfied him, far more so than she had ever pleased her husband, she doubted Kane would want to pursue the subject again so soon. At this point, he'd only granted her the status of roommate—a convenient sexual partner, she supposed.

"Are you hungry?" he asked.

There. She'd known it. To think Kane—or any man—would want to make love to her instead of eating was a farfetched notion at best. "Not particularly," she confessed, her hands dropping to her bare thighs. "You go ahead. I think I'll take a shower."

Kane turned toward her.

Her breath lodged in her lungs the moment she saw the heated look in his eyes. It appeared she had seriously underestimated his interest in sex as well as his ability to recover his powers. Virile did not begin to describe Kane Rainer.

"A shower sounds perfect," he agreed. "We'll take it together."

"Kane, I . . ."

In a single agile motion, he swept her into his arms. On long, easy strides he carried her into the bathroom. "I promise to make it a long, leisurely shower. It may last the rest of the night."

She trembled at the blatantly indecent images that came to mind. Her. Kane. Slick and wet as the steam rose around them, their bodies joined in an intimate mating. "Don't you . . . have to go back on patrol?"

"I called in sick."

Sometime later, she nuzzled against Kane's shoulder, wondering at the ease with which he aroused her to previously unknown heights of passion. It was as though she'd been living the life of a nun, sheltered from what a man and a woman could share together. And now, at last, she'd been given a taste of that precious experience.

"Margo, sweetheart..."

"Hmm," she responded dreamily, stretching a little on his bed, not wanting to break the spell.

"There's something else you have a right to know."

A knot tightened in the pit of her stomach. She wouldn't ask. She'd burrow her way into sleep and wouldn't hear the words she somehow knew would give her nightmares, probably for the rest of her life.

"That day I went after Alby at the mortuary... I remember enough about what happened to know... right that minute... I wanted my brother dead. I was mad enough that I wanted to kill him."

His words hung in the air with an ugly wash of reality, like bed sheets blackened by coal dust that wouldn't come clean.

Kane waited for Margo's response. He'd told her everything now. He was as vulnerable as a man could get, the dark secret of his soul as bare as his butt. If she couldn't handle that, there wasn't much point in going on. Maybe he didn't deserve to.

Her hand rested lightly on his chest, right where a profound ache had been building as he made his confession. Her head was resting on his shoulder. She smelled of the same wintergreen soap he'd been using for years. On her it reminded him of springtime.

"Kane, you're not a killer." Her whispered words spread across his soul like a healing balm. "If you were, I'd know."

"How?" How could she, when he still questioned the truth.

"Because..." She hesitated, making Kane worry she was about to change her mind. "Because you are a good man and I think you always have been."

He sat on the edge of the bed, looking out the window for a long time after Margo drifted off to sleep. The mortuary was quiet now. Or at least there wasn't any blue-green glow visible.

But Kane had made *it* angry. He could feel the animosity radiating from across the street as though it were a living thing. Enraged waves of hate undulated toward him. He could feel them searing his skin and aching painfully in his gut as though he'd been invaded by an army of deadly maggots.

I'm gonna get you for this! She wanted to play with me!

His hands closed into fists. Stopping the green mist would force him to face his brother's death all over again. This time, Kane would know for sure if he was the murderer.

* * *

He'd withdrawn from her.

Margo had sensed it all morning in the taut way he held himself and the fine lines of stress around his eyes. They'd eaten breakfast in a silence made loud with words that were unspoken. Then, when she insisted she had to go to work, he escorted her to the mortuary to open the doors for the remodeling crew.

Perhaps Kane felt he'd allowed himself to become too vulnerable in her eyes. Too human. He definitely wasn't the kind of man who relished admitting weakness. Not that his guilt about his brother's death seemed anything but normal to Margo. She carried around a lot of remorse, too, for deeds of both omission and commission.

"Good morning, you two." A smiling Penelope stepped out from behind the private patio entrance to the mortuary. "Looks like it might be a shade or two cooler today." She squinted up at a wispy trail of marine clouds already beginning to dissipate. "My voices like it best when it ain't so hot."

"We all do," Margo agreed.

"Did you sleep in there last night?" Kane questioned with no-nonsense cop talk, indicating the patio and its small, weedy garden and a spindly liquidambar tree that would have benefited from a good dose of water.

Penelope's rheumy eyes took in his aggressive stance. "I keep on the move, mister, and don't harm nobody."

"It's not safe to hang around the mortuary," he insisted. "So find someplace else to crash or I'll see you picked up for loitering."

Margo tried to intercede. "I wish you'd let me find you a bed—"

"I gotta be on my way." Penelope hefted her shopping bags, balancing their weight evenly with one in each hand. "Bernice says I can visit Algernon anytime I want. She's being right nice about it."

"Don't let me catch you here again," Kane warned as Penelope shuffled off down the sidewalk.

Instinctively, Margo reached out to place a calming hand on his arm. He flinched at her touch and she pulled away as though her fingers had been burned.

"Don't go soft-soap social worker on me, Margo. You know damn well it's dangerous for *anyone* to be around this mortuary, particularly at night." His eyes narrowed. "Your bag-lady friend could get herself killed."

"I know." Or after what had happened last night, she should have known. Yet in the bright light of day, it all seemed so unreal. Could she have actually heard Kane talking to the mist? It must have been her imagination.

"If you read the autopsy report on the John Doe they found in the mortuary, you know the body was never identified. The coroner speculated the deceased had been dead for years, and perhaps left in the old mortuary as some grotesque practical joke."

"I suppose that's possible."

"Not very likely when you read the list describing the contents of his pockets. He had a 1994 nickel on him, Margo. In nearly mint condition."

Shuddering, Margo realized the victim couldn't have been dead for long when his body was discovered.

Desiccated cadaver. Mummified body. Stomach and bowel entirely empty of residue. No visible cause of death.

She looked up at the building that should have been benign and wasn't that at all. White stucco. A false Spanish tile roof. Windows with ordinary square panes gazing blandly back at her. And she knew Kane was right. Penelope Fairweather should stay as far away from the mortuary as her tired legs could take her.

"I want you to go with me today," he said.

Margo turned to Kane. His white T-shirt was almost as bright as the whitewashed stucco she'd just been staring at. "Go where with you?"

"To find some answers."

"I've at least got to get the workmen started."

"I'll wait."

From the determined set of his jaw, Margo had the distinct impression Kane wanted her along as much to keep her safely away from the mortuary basement as to provide him with assistance. She supposed she should be pleased. Instead, she was slightly irritated with his imperious attitude.

But she suppressed her irritation. She needed to get some answers, too.

A dozen reference books were stacked at the end of the library study table and the senior librarian for Southwest Museum was somewhere on the second floor searching for more tomes on Native Americans indigenous to the Torrance and South Bay area of the Los Angeles basin.

"This isn't exactly like researching the Sioux," Margo said, flipping open a heavy volume on California Indians. "The Gabrielinos weren't very well-known, at least not before Father Serra founded the local mission."

The corners of Kane's lips kicked up. "The missionaries probably co-opted the Gabrielinos' PR man right off and put a lid on any adverse publicity. That's what the marines always do."

Margo repressed a smile. Away from Torrance—and the mortuary—Kane seemed more relaxed. He had a dry, if slightly twisted, sense of humor that was quite appealing. Along with assorted other admirable attributes, she thought with an inaudible sigh.

"It looks like there were several Indian villages on the Palos Verdes Peninsula," Margo said, returning to her reading. "Most of them on the ocean side."

"Is that where you lived?"

Her head snapped up. Sometimes she nearly forgot about her other life, a slightly indulged one where she made no decisions, was pampered in many ways and was always totally dependent upon the whims of her husband. "We had a view of Santa Monica Bay and the basin. It was lovely."

"Do you miss it?"

"The view? I suppose. For the rest..." She shook her head. "Only my children."

He held her gaze for a moment, something hot and needy in his eyes. Then, apparently satisfied with her response, he returned to his own reading. Lord, he was a hard man to understand. This morning he'd acted as if they hadn't made love together—that it had been nothing more than a good roll in the hay. But since then, she'd caught him looking at her furtively and the anguish in his eyes had almost taken her breath away.

Clearly, she didn't have enough experience with men to deal with Kane Rainer.

"Here's something odd," he said.

She roused herself from her sensual reveries. "What's that?"

"There was a creek in what's now Torrance that the Indians called the Black Creek."

"Black? That doesn't sound like a particularly scenic creek, unless..." She cocked her head. "Oil, maybe. The whole of Torrance is on top of one huge oil field. Even in that nice residential area of Marble Estates, every tenth lot is an oil well pumping away and the oil companies are doing a lot of slant drilling."

"I know. And it sounds like this Black Creek might have been over by Torrance Elementary School. A winter creek, I imagine, 'cause there wouldn't be enough water for a year-round flow."

"That's pretty near downtown but it must be entirely dried-up now. Just a wash, maybe. And certainly no oil oozing up to the surface."

"Yeah. According to this story, the Indians wouldn't go anywhere near the place. They were real superstitious about it until after..." He hesitated, obviously reading ahead. "An electrical storm! Dammit, I should have known."

"What are you talking about?"

"Twice now I've given that green mist a jolt of electricity. Minor in terms of voltage, but both times it's backed off." He jabbed the page with his finger. "This says, according to legend, there was an unusually powerful electrical storm that frightened all of the villagers on the Palos Verdes Peninsula. After that, the Indians weren't afraid of Black Creek anymore."

"Do you suppose the lightning set the surface oil on fire? That might explain what happened."

"Possibly." He looked across the table at her, his eyes narrowing once again and filling with an evangelist's fervor. "But I think it may be even more complicated than that."

CHAPTER TEN

"I think the mist—whatever it is—comes from somewhere in the earth's mantle, between the earth's surface and the molten core." As casually as he'd made his pronouncement, Kane sprinkled salt liberally over the heap of French fries on his plate, then added catsup.

They'd stopped at a coffee shop for dinner on the way back to Torrance from the Southwest Museum. He'd ordered a double-double cheeseburger and fries, plus a cola. Margo had chosen a chicken salad. Kane was a very basic kind of guy, she mused, absolutely no pretensions, and quite a contrast to her ex. Royce had forever been trying to impress his business associates with his knowledge of fine wines and continental cuisine. But never once had she seen Royce enjoy his fancy meals the way Kane relished a simple hamburger.

Her boys had been much the same as Kane. She hoped they still were and wished, no doubt fruitlessly, that Richard and Steve would have a chance to meet him.

Although she would have preferred to contemplate Kane's many admirable qualities, Margo forced herself to concentrate on a far less pleasant topic—the killing force in the mortuary.

"Why from the middle of the earth?" she asked.

"You've smelled it. It's got to be composed of decaying vegetation—organic matter."

Putrid and ugly, enough decomposing funeral flowers to reach to the center of the earth? In some bizarre way it might be metaphysically possible, she conceded. "You think it's something as simple as methane gas? Like they get at landfills?"

"That might account for the green glow, like swamp gas, but I don't think that's the whole explanation. And the mist doesn't appear to be explosive like methane, or I would have already blown up the place with the electrical shot from my taser."

That didn't exactly create a pretty picture. The mortuary—Kane and Margo included—blown to smithereens all over downtown Torrance. She shuddered, and tried to blame her shiver on the restaurant's overactive air conditioner. The truth was, her imagination had been cruising along in high gear for some time.

"And methane gas doesn't draw bodily fluids from passersby," he added.

She shoved her salad away. Food held little interest at the moment; her stomach was far too unsettled.

"You got excited when you read about Black Creek. What's that got to do with anything?"

"Because the Black probably was seeping oil and when I read that, things began to fall into place. Oil is formed from decaying matter, both animal and vegetable. Right?"

She nodded.

"What if the weight of the earth's crust forms other compounds that we don't even know about yet because they're created even deeper in the mantle than oil? Some that aren't as benign as oil. And maybe they even *feed* on the decaying vegetation down there."

"Oh, Kane, that's sickening."

"Yeah, maybe, but maggots feed on decaying flesh. That's what nature intended them to do. Who's to say there aren't other creatures that have similar roles in the grand scheme of things?

"Then, let's say, we go around drilling holes in the earth's crust, trying to recover all that economically important oil. Or earthquakes—like the one in Long Beach in '35—shake things up. And bingo, some kind of a path to the surface occurs. And our nasty green mist comes up and discovers a whole new world. One that doesn't have any ready-made food for it. And so, because survival is absolutely basic, it learns how to find nourishment on its own."

Following his line of reasoning, she said, "And this *thing* that comes up out of the ground manages to turn bodily fluids into the gaseous compound we see."

"Probably by using heat. I'd guess below the surface it's even hotter than what we feel in the building."

"It all makes a hideous sort of sense," she agreed. "But it doesn't explain ... we've both heard voices, Kane. You say it's your brother, and I guess I can't argue with that. Very likely all ten-year-old boys sound alike. But how ... how would a gaseous substance develop a voice?"

He turned pale beneath his ruddy complexion and he shoved his unfinished hamburger aside as if his appetite had fled. "I think ... somehow ... it absorbed Alby's personality and is using that to lure food to it."

"But why Alby and not one of the vagrants? Or even Poopsie, for that matter?"

"Who knows? Maybe it's because my brother was more intrinsically evil than an innocent dog or some poor slob who was just looking for a place to sleep. Or maybe the mist is getting smarter about how to attract food. It could be evolving."

"This all sounds so incredible. Evolution?"

"When the mist made its way up to the mortuary, nutrients were readily available from the corpses that were brought in. Maybe the scent is what drew it in the first place. Now it has to work harder to survive. It's *learning*."

"Oh, God..." Her stomach did one of those unpleasant rolls, as if she were riding Colossus at Magic Mountain.

"There are some very large cracks in the basement floor of the mortuary. I noticed them the first time I went down there."

"Yes." Grotesque serpentine fissures yawning like an open abyss into the unknown.

"And that apprentice mortician who showed up the day after Poopsie died started on the job at the mortuary just the day before one of the biggest earthquakes that's hit L.A. in modern history."

"Kane..." She tried to take a drink of iced tea, but her hand trembled so violently she had to set the glass back down. "Do you think Penelope is hearing the same voice we've been hearing? And it's trying to lure—"

He covered her hand with long, strong, capable fingers. "I know you think I've been tough on that old bag lady, but she doesn't deserve to die any more than anyone else does. My job is to keep her safe. And that means keeping her away from the mortuary."

"So what are we going to do?"

He went back to work on his French fries, eating them slowly, thoughtfully.

"Kane? What are you thinking? Surely you're not planning to—" She sought for a word, trying to avoid the one that came instantly to mind. *Killer. Killer.*

Kane's a killer! "— to try to get rid of the mist all on your own?"

With stubborn concentration, he ignored her question.

"I'm not going to let you do that. This isn't *Star Wars* and you can't turn your taser gun into a laser sword and go off to fight the dark forces of the world. You're not Luke Skywalker, you don't have to be a hero and that *thing* at the mortuary isn't Darth Vader. You could get killed!"

He looked at her then, a spark of amusement in his eyes like sun glistening off of steel. "How did you know that was my favorite movie?"

"Oh, please..." She groaned.

"I think there's a way to put that thing out of commission and do it without risking my neck. But I can't talk about it."

"Because it's a secret? Or because you know I'll tell you you're nuts?"

He shrugged. "A little of both, I suppose."

She hated people who gave evasive answers.

"It may take me a couple of days to arrange things," he said. "And I'll have to pull a lot of strings."

"Strings?" A flutter of gooseflesh stroked down her spine. Something secret. Given Kane's military background, maybe something high-tech and classified. She'd heard about spook-projects in the aerospace business that were so far-out they went beyond science fiction.

"Meanwhile, first thing tomorrow, I want you to start moving your gear out of the mortuary."

"Are you going to blow the place up, after all?"

"If it comes to that."

Nothing Kane had told Margo was very reassuring. When all was said and done, there might not be a homeless shelter in Torrance. After all the work and politicking that had been done to make the shelter possible, the project could easily go up in smoke. Or worse, be so unsafe no one could live there.

With her fingertips, she rubbed at the niggling headache threatening at her temple. Why couldn't she simply enjoy the thrill of being Kane's lover—for however long he showed an interest—and explore more fully the sensual experience he'd revealed to her? Was that really so much for a farm girl from Iowa to ask?

Nothing in her background had prepared her to deal with noxious green mists that creep up from the bowels of the earth to kill people.

Her chest ached with the possibility of another defeat in a life that had been filled with more failures than she cared to admit. "Maybe we should both just walk away from it."

"I can't. It's got a hold of my brother."

* * *

Margo eyed the mortuary as they drove past. It brooded there on the shadowed street corner, a symbol of death. The impending sense of loss weighed heavily in the air, like gathering storm clouds, and clogged Margo's throat with fear.

Kane's going to die! Tee-hee. Can't stop me!

She folded her arms tight across her stomach and fought against the press of tears at the backs of her eyes. Her noble hero was going to duel with evil, perhaps to the death. She had no way to stop him, and no right to try. He'd carried the burden of his brother's death for a long time. He needed a chance to bring an end to the torment it had cost him.

Parking behind Margo's car, Kane nuzzled his civilian car bumper-to-bumper with the Cadillac. The Brazilian peppertree at the curbside had shed a dirty blanket of leaves across the parked vehicle. Idly, as though thinking about the mundane would allow her to forget the unimaginable, she wondered when on earth she'd have a chance to wash her car.

Kane switched off the ignition but made no move to get out, simply staring straight ahead instead.

"When you were living in your car, weren't you afraid?"

"Sometimes," she admitted. "I always locked my doors and made it a point to park in neighborhoods that were safe."

"There's no neighborhood that's entirely safe."

"My biggest fear was that somebody would spot the car one too many times in the neighborhood and call the cops. I didn't want to get arrested." That surely would have been the final degradation. Being home-less was bad enough. The humiliation of being booked and fingerprinted would have been more than she could bear. "I pretty much kept on the move and never slept very soundly."

He slanted her a glance. The overhanging limbs of the tree shaded the car and little light penetrated the interior. "It must have been hell." His voice was rough-edged with sympathy.

"I wouldn't want to go through it again."

"Next time I roust one of those bums that sleep in doorways, I'll keep that in mind."

It was a small concession, Margo realized, but one that suggested Kane was learning poverty didn't nec-essarily equate with stupidity.

Something about the way Kane continued to look at her, or maybe the way he was holding himself so taut, suddenly made Margo feel hot. A wave of sensuality washed over her and something deep inside her shim-mered in anticipation. She'd never met a man who was so innately sexual. Tendrils of need curled through her midsection, instinctively responding to his unspoken message, and she marveled at their awesome power.

"Yoo-hoo! Kane! Is that you, young man?"

In unison, Kane and Margo turned toward the chilling sound of Mrs. Cornelius's voice.

Kane flicked open the door and light flooded the interior darkness of the car. "What can we do for you, Mrs. Cornelius?"

"It's my little puppy. Algernon dug his way out from under the fence and I'm so afraid. Oh, my, do you think—"

Margo met Kane's eyes without making any effort to disguise her fear. Neither did he.

They were both out of the car an instant later. Kane with a flashlight in his hand. Swearing. Margo right behind him. Running toward the mortuary.

Here doggy, doggy. Come see what I have for you.

Margo cringed and fought the bile that rose in her throat. This couldn't be happening again!

It wasn't fair to Mrs. Cornelius. She loved that little dog almost as much as she had loved Poopsie.

Suddenly, from out of the shadows a puppy bounded into the street to join in the fray. He yapped and his tail wagged, all joy and good fun. He dashed through Kane's legs and leaped up on Margo's thigh.

She nearly collapsed in relief.

"Oh, what a naughty, naughty boy you've been." Hurrying to retrieve her pet, Mrs. Cornelius scooped Algernon into her arms. Squirming, he licked her face and nuzzled his nose against the old woman's neck. She hugged him back. Fiercely. "Now, babykins, you're going to get a spank-spank if you're bad again. You mustn't dig up Mommy's nice roses. We'll just go back home and I'll . . ."

Mrs. Cornelius continued to admonish her dog as she walked back to her house, her voice more cooing than stern, as if she were unaware of the potential consequences of her dog running away.

Margo's shoulders sagged. Her breathing came in ragged gasps and her heart lunged erratically against her ribs. Dear God...

"Let's get back to my place," Kane urged. He cupped her elbow in a distinctly domineering way. "I've got a lot of calls to make."

Kane shut himself in his bedroom. He was about to call in every favor that had ever been owed him, from generals on down. And if they weren't willing to help, by damn, he'd violate every security rule in the book. He'd *kill* Albert Joshua Rainer, favored son of Marsha and Henry, and this time they'd damn well thank him.

He snatched up the phone from beside the bed.

Damn, he wished he could remember what had happened that night at the mortuary. There had been snatches of memories in his head—Alby's screams, the kid's face contorted with fear and an agonizing veil that had descended to obscure his vision. But the pieces didn't fit together. It was like grasping a handful of sand and having it all run through his fingers.

Neener-Neener! Can't catch meee!

"I'm gonna get you this time, Alby. And I'm gonna blow you to hell 'n' gone."

Kane dropped his head into his hand and heaved a dry sob. A ten-year-old snot-nosed kid shouldn't have had to die.

Margo curled up on her side on the lower bunk. She'd gotten ready for bed because it was late and she didn't know what else to do. But she didn't want to be here alone, with *KILLER* inscribed above her head, and not knowing what Kane was up to. She wanted to feel his arms around her, the hard, long heat of him within her. And she had no right to ask for any of that.

She could still hear his muted voice through the walls. A dozen calls. Maybe more. Arranging God knew what kind of hideous device that would destroy the green mist. Or Kane, himself.

She wished she hadn't seen the dark shadows lurking in the depths of his eyes. The residue of pain and anguish. A darkness that flickered around the edges of his machismo, witness to the cruelty he had experienced as a child—a cruelty that might easily have driven a weaker man to murder.

But not Kane. God help her, if Kane was a killer, she didn't want to know.

Doubts gnawed away at her like acid on granite. Slowly. Painfully. Searing into her consciousness even as she fought against a truth she didn't dare face.

Kane could have killed his brother.

And left him there, lifeless, a corpse delivered into the grasp of a force that voraciously consumed bodily fluids from cadavers. That fed on them. Hungering in obscene need of nourishment.

"Oh, God . . ."

Ally-ally-oxen-free! Why don't you come out and play with me?

The door to her room swung open, spilling a rectangle of light across the threshold. The jeans-clad silhouette in the doorway was big and very masculine, compelling.

"I figure that bunk bed's gonna give us a real problem." Kane's low, raspy voice skidded along every one of Margo's nerve endings, touching her psyche at some basic level. "If we make love on the bottom, I'll probably bounce my skull on the top bunk. And if we do it on top, we're both likely to fall off and seriously hurt ourselves, assuming we'd fit with all that junk up there."

He extended his hand. "I need you, Margo. Maybe more than I've ever needed anyone in my life."

She'd never been able to resist anyone who needed her. Tonight was no exception.

She forgot she had doubts about Kane. Deeper still, she trusted him. With her heart. With her body. Even with her life, if that's what it took.

She reached out to him with more than just her hand. As she slipped out of the narrow bed and stood, she was more vulnerable than she had ever been in her life—naked in spite of the T-shirt she was wearing. If Kane was the villain, then there was no justice anywhere on this earth. And in spite of all that had happened to her, Margo hadn't yet given up on that.

He took her hand, drawing her close. For long moments they stood silently, their bodies brushing, aching breasts against rock-hard chest, thigh against thigh. She felt the stirring of his arousal pressing low on her belly. The room filled with the whispered sound of their rhythmic breathing. Settling around them like a velvet blanket, the night air embraced them. The whole house seemed to sigh as Kane finally dipped his head to cover Margo's mouth with his.

She felt the warm moistness of his lips and tongue echo much lower in her body. Her body pulsated with awareness. She melted against him. At the back of her throat, she felt a moan of pleasure forming and smiled a secret smile. For tonight, she could give what Kane needed and accept the satisfaction that he offered in return.

When his hand slipped under the T-shirt to cup Margo's breast, the tension within her began to mount. His callused fingers worked hot magic on her nipple.

She wrapped her arms around his neck. Spearing her fingers through the hair at his nape, she felt the silken strands curl and wave, capturing her in a web of hedonistic pleasure. No man had ever made her feel this way. Feminine. Desirable. *Sexy*.

When he broke the kiss, his eyes were nearly black with sensual need. He groaned, "Oh, baby, you're so hot."

"It's what you do to me. I can't seem to..." His thumb flicked roughly over her nipple and he ground his pelvis against hers. "...catch my breath."

He grinned with pure masculine arrogance.

"Think we could lie down somewhere?" she asked. It didn't much matter where. Her legs felt so weak and rubbery, on the floor would have done fine, but he led her to his room.

He took the time to toss the blankets aside and slip out of his clothes. The sheets felt cool and smelled of the wintergreen scent of his soap. He lay down beside her. Slowly, his palm smoothed across her stomach, then dipped lower. She bucked against his hand.

"Kane!" Heat shimmered through her.

"Yeah, baby. It's okay."

"Let me..." Words escaped her, but she let her actions speak for her instead. She closed her hand around the hard length of him.

Kane jerked sharply. "Yes..."

She gloried in the shudder that passed between them. Stroking him again, she tangled her fingers in the dark mass of hair that curled at the base of his sleek male flesh. When his thighs separated, she explored further, cupping him gently.

On a harsh intake of air, Kane rolled above her. "Enough..."

He entered her swiftly, making her gasp at the unbearable pleasure. Her hips rolled. He slipped deeper into her, growing even larger, and stroking her with a fierce wildness that spoke of his need and years of loneliness. Margo responded in kind, letting go of her insecurities and erasing her doubts.

She scored his back with her fingernails and wrapped her legs around his hips, meeting each of his powerful thrusts with a matching one of her own.

The tension burst on a rolling surge that brought a guttural roar of satisfaction from Kane and the sob of his name to Margo's lips.

A smile climbed Margo's cheeks as she woke in the morning, and grew broader while she dressed for the day. Whenever she happened to be near Kane, they reached out to touch each other. A quick brush of fingers, or a lingering kiss.

By unspoken mutual agreement, they ignored the dark threat that loomed at the mortuary. Instead, they wrapped themselves in a fantasy made for lovers, the sweet bliss of the morning after. A leisurely breakfast. The lazy meeting of a heated gaze over the rim of a coffee mug that rekindled memories. They stole the time together, pretending it would last forever. And knowing the moment of reckoning would arrive all too soon.

She sneaked a look at the kitchen clock. The minute hand seemed to be speeding toward the hour.

"I have to open up for the workmen," she said.

"I know."

"Maybe I'll have a chance to work on my résumé today."

"I want you packed and out of there. Before dinner."

"You're bossy."

His lips twitched. "Yeah. You mind?"

"It bothers me some." Not as much as it should, she realized, but domineering men were still on her list of guys to avoid.

"I'll come with you to the mortuary."

"You don't have to."

"But I'm pushy." He bent over and kissed her at the juncture of her neck and shoulder, sending a delicious shudder of longing right to her nether regions. "And you smell too good to leave alone with the hired hands."

He didn't say anything about the green mist. Or the danger. It was all part of their pretense.

They crossed the street together, the tips of their fingers just touching. Margo's low-heeled pumps clicked a steady beat on the asphalt and Kane shortened his stride to keep pace with her. The downtown stores weren't open yet for business; no tempting bouquets marked the doorway of the florist and the traffic was light. Down the street, a line of supplicants had gathered at the state employment office waiting for the moment the doors would open.

At the big double doors of the mortuary, Margo slid the key into the lock and pushed it open.

I win! You lose the game!

Putrid air slammed into her lungs. Rank as an outhouse, foul as a garbage dump. Her first breath gagged her. Her stomach knotted and she covered her mouth with her hand for fear she would throw up.

There, in the middle of the vestibule, tattooed with the reds and greens and yellows of reflected sunlight cast through the stained-glass window, lay a pile of what looked to be old rags. A shopping bag rested at either side of the heap like two grotesque monuments.

A scream rose in Margo's throat. It scraped at the tender tissue like jagged razor blades.

"Penelope . . ."

CHAPTER ELEVEN

Shell-shocked.

Kane had seen the symptoms among green troops in the Gulf War. Now that distant, unfocused look was in Margo's eyes, the slight tremor in her hands. And he swore under his breath, savagely, as if that would make any difference. No one could come back easily from the shock she had experienced.

In an odd way, Penelope Fairweather had been Margo's friend, he realized—maybe even her mission.

The rotating ambulance light swept crimson across Margo's cheeks as she sat on the porch steps of the mortuary. From inside the building, fans blew the foul stench of death out onto the street through open windows and doors. Homicide detectives prowled through the place and asked questions while the blue suits strung yellow tape to cordon off the scene.

Beyond the yellow tape, a crowd of curious neighbors gathered as though they were waiting for a circus act to perform. Mothers out for their morning walks pushed strollers across the street past clutches of laughing high-school kids who should have been in class. Toddlers shrieked as they momentarily escaped on their own, only to be corralled again by over-wrought moms.

Kane knew all of the police efforts were useless. They weren't going to discover the bag lady's murderer any more than they had figured out who—or what—had killed Alby. Because they wouldn't listen to Kane.

His gut twisted on ancient memories, and ones that were only hours old.

A police officer stepped out of the building, wiped his face with his hand and tipped his hat to the back of his head.

"Man, somebody sure turned that old lady to crispy beef jerky," he said. Louie's pockmarked face shifted into an ugly caricature of a fat cop. "The old biddy looks like my girl does when she spends too much time out in the sun."

"Knock it off, Louie," Kane said grimly, hating the man who'd been a bully since their high-school days.

"Don't get yourself exercised, Kane. Unless you had somethin' to do with that old broad dying."

To Louie's sneering comment, Kane replied with a muttered, "Up yours."

"Hell, it doesn't matter. She was just an old bag lady that nobody'll miss. The city's better rid of her. It's one way to clean up the streets."

Margo leaped to her feet, animated for the first time since they'd found Penelope's body.

Jabbing Officer Louie Marconi in the chest with her finger, Margo drove him back a step. "I'll miss her, dammit! Penelope Fairweather was a good woman. She had children, you know. She was a *mother*. And she loved dogs—" Her voice caught on a sob. "She was sick, that's all. It can happen to anyone."

Kane wrapped his arms around her. "Easy, babe. Don't let Louie get to you. He hasn't got half the sense God gave him, and that wasn't much to begin with."

Turning in Kane's arms, she leaned into him, burying her face in his chest. Her delicate body heaved with the sobs she tried to muffle. "The workmen left the side door open. I should have checked. It's all my fault...."

He smoothed his hand over her hair. He felt so damn helpless. And she felt so good in his arms. "It's all right, honey. It's better to cry and let it all out." Tears were the best medicine for grief. And guilt. He wished he had some left to shed.

A kid of twenty-something, trailed by an equally young woman draped in professional camera gear, pushed their way through the gathering crowd.

"Daily Breeze," the young fellow announced, flipping open one of those little spiral notebooks and pulling a nubby pencil from his shirt pocket. "Heard

on the police radio that somebody found a body. I'd like to get a statement, if I can."

The girl unhooked her camera. She was all lanky legs and long hair, wearing jeans and a vest with a zillion pockets.

"You'll have to wait until the press relations officer arrives," Kane interjected before Louie could take center stage.

Almost immediately, Kane noted the arrival of a TV van on the street. He groaned inwardly. This could quickly turn into a media circus. He didn't want Margo to be a part of that, and didn't relish the idea for himself, either. He'd had enough attention years ago when Alby died to last him a lifetime.

A minute later, Lieutenant Ramsey showed up in a black and white, parking it nose in at the curb. His unhurried stride masked a tension far more evident in the ramrod straightness of his spine.

Suddenly, a woman burst out of the crowd and ducked under the yellow tape. "My baby! I can't find my baby!"

Louie stepped in front of the lieutenant. "You can't come in here, lady."

"But my baby," she pleaded. "He was right there and then I turned around and he was gone. I can't find him anywhere. Oh, please, help me. Shane's only three years old."

"The kid's probably hiding in the bushes or somethin', lady. We can't look for every—"

Lieutenant Ramsey spoke low and quick to the officer. Seconds later, three other blue suits had come out front and Kane knew an intensive search for the toddler was about to begin. God, he hoped Alby hadn't lured the poor kid inside the mortuary.

"Lieutenant, Peter Snell of the *Breeze*. Do you think this missing child is in any way connected to—"

The lieutenant ignored the reporter. "Rainer. Ms. Stafford." He nodded to them both. "The city manager would like to see you in his office. Now. I'll drive you to city hall."

"Watch out, Kane." Louie smirked. "They're finally gonna nail ya."

Kane's temper shot to the boiling point and he did what he'd wanted to do for years. He landed a solid right cross to Louie's jaw, driving him backward until he staggered and settled on his butt, looking up at Kane with glazed eyes. Flexing his fingers, Kane decided a few bruised knuckles were a fair trade for finally putting Louie in his place.

As another uniformed officer helped Louie to his feet, the lieutenant caught Kane's arm. "Let's go." There was a warning in his voice not to test his limits too far. "You, too, Ms. Stafford."

"We should be looking for that missing boy," Kane insisted. "The same thing that killed the bag lady could kill—"

Ramsey shook his head. "It's out of your hands now."

"Are we being arrested?" Margo asked, a fine shudder rippling through her body.

"No, ma'am. So far as I know, the city manager and the mayor just want to talk with you both."

"Are these two people under suspicion?" the reporter asked. "And what about the missing kid?"

The photographer snapped a picture.

"You'll get your statement all in due time, Snell," the lieutenant said.

Ramsey expertly escorted Kane and Margo past the reporter to the waiting vehicle. Kane had a very bad feeling about what was going to happen next, both for Margo and himself, as well as the missing toddler. Alby had always reveled in taunting younger children.

Margo pleaded for a few minutes to freshen up and used the ladies' room on the third floor of city hall. The mirror told a dismal story—eyes red-rimmed and filled with despair, hair disheveled and a cotton blouse that looked as if it had been slept in.

She splashed water on her face, straightened her hair as best she could and mentally gave herself a dose of courage. Either the mayor and city manager would listen to their story, or they wouldn't.

Liar, liar, pants on fire! That's what they'll think.

She closed her eyes. How could that awful taunting voice reach into her mind from so far away—unless she was as crazy as Penelope.

The city manager's office looked like a gathering of mourners. The mayor in her power suit with a TV-perfect powder blue blouse. Rumpled, as usual, the city manager had at least managed to pull his tie straight. The police lieutenant was wearing a standard-issue gray suit that contrasted sharply with Kane's off-duty jeans and stenciled T-shirt. He looked particularly grim.

"Ms. Stafford, I believe the city has seriously misplaced its faith in you," the city manager began. "We appreciate that you have been an advocate for the homeless for some time. However, that does not justify negligence."

"Negligence?" she echoed. How was one *careful* about a killing mist?

"That *poor,* poor woman got into the building because you were careless, Ms. Stafford. Doors were not properly secured and, regrettably, that cost a woman her life."

"Margo locked the doors, Mr. Hendrickson," Kane insisted with a lie. "I watched her do it."

"You're wrong, Kane." Guilt thickened in her throat and she wouldn't let him cover for her. "I didn't go back to the mortuary last night after the workmen left. The doors could have been standing wide open, for all I know. Maybe if I had..." Oh, damn, she was going to cry again. For Penelope. And for her own stupidity.

"The front door was locked when we got there this morning," Kane said, still trying to defend her.

"Yes, well..." Hendrickson cleared his throat.

The mayor stood by the windows that looked out over the main boulevard lined with eucalyptus trees. "You must understand, both of you," she said imperiously, "we can't tolerate negative publicity in this community. It's extremely bad for the economy, and that has a dilatory effect on our tax base. Our municipal resources are already stretched to the limit."

"A woman died," Margo said vehemently. "Surely that's more important than—"

"That is, of course, unfortunate," the city manager interrupted, "but not at issue at the moment. I'm afraid we find we can no longer use your services, Ms. Stafford."

"You can't fire her!" Kane bellowed. "What about civil service? You've at least got to have a hearing."

"Officer Rainer." With exaggerated patience, Hendrickson rose from behind his cluttered desk. "Ms. Stafford is well within her probationary period and the city is well within its rights to terminate her employment when we see fit. For cause, in this case."

Margo felt unsteady on her feet. *Fired*. Discharged for incompetence was how her record would read. No reference. Leading to a job hunt that would be unbearably long.

She did a quick mental audit of her bank account and knew she'd be living in her car again all too soon. Whatever Kane had offered in terms of housing would be temporary at best.

Oh, God, her babies! When would she get to see her sweet children?

Frantically, she looked from the city manager to the mayor and back again. They couldn't do this to her. "You don't understand," she pleaded, trying to keep some semblance of control. "There's a green mist in the mortuary. It comes up from deep in the earth and it kills people. That's what happened to Penelope, and Alby, and that vagrant you didn't want anyone to know about...."

They didn't believe her. She could see doubt and pity in their eyes, but no regret that she would be living on the streets again. They simply thought she was crazy. Like Penelope...

"Come on, Margo, let's get out of here."

Kane took her arm. Numbly she followed his lead out of the office. Although they walked purposefully, she caught the odd looks of secretaries and administrative personnel peering out of their posh offices.

She wanted—perversely—to stick out her tongue at them.

She wanted to sob.

Crybaby! Crybaby! Why don't you go on home?

They'd barely made it to the elevator and punched the button before Lieutenant Ramsey showed up.

"Kane, I'm sorry." His eyebrows angled downward, making his expression conform to his words. "Hendrickson's calling the chief. You're going to be put on administrative leave. They're going to blame you for hitting a fellow officer, but we both know the suspension is political. The mayor's afraid you're going to undermine her pet project and maybe even cost her an election."

For a moment, Kane hesitated, then the rugged lines of his face turned to granite. In those hard, unyielding features Margo could see a lifetime etched with rejection. The kid who had never been accepted in any group. Until the marines, she imagined. Still, he'd given up the sense of belonging he must surely have experienced in the corps to return to Torrance and face his demons.

She doubted there was any man more courageous than Kane Rainer.

"Tell the chief not to bother. You'll have my resignation on your desk by the end of the workday."

Nodding, Ramsey said, "I didn't want it to end this way."

"I know. I never should have come back." Kane extended his hand. "Any word on the missing toddler?"

The two men shook hands, tall and strong, a meeting of professionals who respected each other. "Not yet. I checked. We searched the building and came up empty. We figure the kid may be playing hide-and-seek in some of the alleys around there. We've rounded up the Explorer Scouts to conduct a search. They'll find him."

"I hope so," Kane said, ushering Margo into the open elevator.

Margo's spirits sank with the double blow. A missing child to distract the police from the real evil that lurked in the mortuary. And now, since he'd quit his job, there was no longer any reason for Kane to stay in Torrance. And she had nowhere else to go.

Suddenly, she felt cold. And alone. More alone than she had felt in a very long time.

The stale air in the elevator smelled vaguely of unwashed bodies, or maybe it was the scent of anxious constituents who had ridden to the third floor to plead their case with the city's top brass.

As the elevator door slid closed, Kane stood rigidly at attention, staring straight ahead, doing his best to absorb this latest blow, she decided. Without looking at her, he said, "I'll help you get your things out of the mortuary."

The elevator shuddered as it began its slow descent.

"It won't take long to pack. I haven't even thrown the boxes away yet."

"You can store your stuff at my place."

She wanted a home, a place to call her own. And, yes, dammit, she wanted this man to love. Not just an impersonal storage warehouse.

Somewhere within her sense of grief and loss, the spark of anger struck sharply against her fears. She deserved more than this. That stupid green mist had desiccated her hopes as surely as it had destroyed Penelope and poor, sick little Poopsie. She didn't like the feeling of metaphorically being its next victim.

Lifting her chin, she said, "At least something good has come out of Penelope's death."

Kane cut her a startled look. "How do you figure that?"

"You've been vindicated, Kane. There is no way you could have killed Penelope. If anyone asks, I can absolutely swear you never left the house last night. And it follows that you weren't the one who killed the vagrants, or Poopsie, or even your brother. They may not believe the green mist exists, but they can't go on blaming you for something you didn't do."

He stared at her incredulously. Slowly, like crumbling shale slipping from the side of a granite mountain, his features rearranged themselves and formed the most devastating smile she had ever seen. He tipped his head back and laughed. Loudly. The full-bodied sound bounced around inside the elevator.

She grinned foolishly at him, her heart expanding in her chest like a birthday balloon.

The door opened on the first floor and two startled city employees stepped out of the way.

"You're wonderful!" In an easy gesture of possession, Kane looped his arm around her shoulders and escorted her out of the elevator. "The world is tumbling down around our heads, something bizarre is killing people and we've both just been canned. In all of that, you can still find something good."

"But it's true! You're absolutely innocent and now you can prove it."

He gave her a quick, hard kiss that held the promise of more to come. "Let's see if we can hitch a ride back home from some cop who's eager to see the last of me."

Eerily quiet.

Their footsteps echoed on the bare wooden floors of the mortuary as though they had entered a place of vast emptiness. The silence seemed to expand beyond the walls. Perhaps into the depths of the earth.

"It's sleeping."

Kane's words stroked a shiver through Margo. The workmen had been told not to cross the yellow tape barriers and had been sent home for the day. The police officers had gone, too, leaving an empty building filled only with the haunting specter of death.

"Does that mean we have to tiptoe around so it doesn't wake up?" she asked.

"It's always more active at night."

Or when it was in search of a good meal, she thought with ghoulish revulsion.

As they climbed the stairs, Margo averted her eyes from the spot where they'd discovered Penelope's body. She didn't check out the stained-glass window, either. Everything in this building had turned ugly. She simply wanted to pack her things and leave.

Kane carried the first few boxes downstairs, boxes she hadn't yet unpacked.

He returned while she was stripping the sheets from the bed she'd never slept in.

"You ever get this cupboard door open?" he asked.

She shook her head. "There are a lot of things I never got around to." Like providing a safe place where homeless women could get back on their feet. Like having a man return the love she was all too willing to give.

When she turned around, she discovered Kane with his palm pressed against the locked door. A muscle worked at his jaw.

Apprehension burrowed into her midsection. "What are you thinking, Kane?"

"I think I don't like locked doors." He glanced around the room. "I don't suppose you have anything like a crowbar?"

"Not likely."

His scowl deepened. "Will you be okay while I go get one?"

"What do you think is in there?"

You can't have it. It's mine!

Margo's whole body jerked as though she'd been shot. "Did you hear—"

"It's awake again." He grabbed her hand, dragging her out of the room and down the stairs.

"What are you doing?"

"I'm getting something that will open that door."

"We should call someone."

"There's no time. It may already be too late."

Kane left her standing on the porch and dashed across the street. Seconds later he reappeared, carrying a crowbar and a long-handled ax.

"Wait here," he ordered as he ran past her.

"Not on your life, buster." She followed him inside and up the stairs. She wasn't going to leave Kane alone. He'd been fighting his demons without backup for too long. This time she'd be there to help.

Wood splintered with a crash. Kane buried the head of the ax into the cupboard door a second time, making the entire building shudder.

Go away!

Kane wrenched a chunk of wood free.

That's not fair. Leave it alone!

With an almost human groan, the hinges broke away from the wall. Plywood, plaster and paint chips fell to the floor and the putrid scent of decay rose from the black hole that appeared. Cloyingly sweet and rancid.

"There's nothing there," Margo protested. A dark shaft to nowhere.

"It's a dumbwaiter." Kane leaned into the darkness, into the fetid hole and its foul smell. "Down to the basement."

"Oh, God..."

Kane overhanded a rope, his arm muscles flexing and straining. A pulley squeaked, the old equipment reluctant to budge after so many years of disuse.

Get lost, ape-nose!

"Shut up, Alby."

You can't make me.

"Oh, yes, I can." Kane grunted as he hauled the weight of the dumbwaiter upward.

With the opening too small for two to work, Margo could do little more than peer over his shoulder. And try to keep her terror at bay. A prayer might have helped, but the words simply wouldn't come.

The top of the dumbwaiter appeared, inching up with each pull on the rope. The increasingly powerful scent of decaying flowers came with it.

Adjusting his position, and blocking Margo's view in the process, Kane strained to get the interior box aligned with the opening of the door. His breathing was ragged.

Something clicked into place.

Kane swore.

"What is it?" Dread licked through her.

He turned around and his sweat-sheened face was ashen. "You can call 911 now."

Looking past him, Margo saw an object about two feet high propped against the back wall of the dumbwaiter. She frowned, trying to make out its shape. From this distance it looked like a giant butterfly cocoon wrapped in silken threads the color of a sea green lagoon.

"Is that..." A basic instinct to deny the first thought that came to mind closed her throat tightly around the unspoken words.

Kane retrieved a knife from his pocket and pried the object open. Sliding the blade under the threads, he ripped the shroud from bottom to top. Slowly, a tiny pair of red sneakers appeared, short, chubby legs and little blue shorts.

"Oh, God, no, Kane. Please..."

He bent over the macabre chrysalis.

"Geez..." His body shuddered and suddenly he seemed driven to furious action. Yanking the child roughly out of the green shroud, he lifted the little boy in his arms. "The kid's alive, Margo. Barely breathing, but alive. Get an ambulance. Now!"

Tears of relief sprang to Margo's eyes as she raced for the phone. She dialed, and in her mind she heard a laugh, a cackle that was only marginally sane, and sounded suspiciously like Penelope Fairweather.

CHAPTER TWELVE

"Will the little boy be all right?" Huddled off to the side of the vestibule, Margo fought the lingering vibrato of fear that racked her body. Kane's strength and his arms wrapped securely around her helped to dampen the terror.

"It looks to me like the paramedics have everything under control."

Admittedly, the child had regained consciousness and was crying fretfully, but Margo still couldn't shake off the horrible sight of the toddler encased in the green cocoon.

"Why?" she asked. "Why would that *thing* wrap up the child and stuff him in a closet?"

"My guess is it's acting on instinct. Some insects capture their prey, then protect it in some way and keep it around to consume later. Since it had just fed on Penelope . . . I think the mist is making adaptations to its environment."

"Oh, dear heavens . . . it was going to eat the child later." Another shudder convulsed Margo and she leaned her head against Kane's shoulder. He felt rock-solid but even a powerful man couldn't fight the green mist all by himself. "We've got to do something, Kane. We can't let that creature go on killing babies."

"Let's go back to my place. I'll make some more phone calls. My contacts have got to agree to help now or, I swear, I'll blow the whistle on them, national security be damned."

He slid his arm around her waist.

They reached the porch to discover an impromptu press conference in progress, Mayor Marian Westcott presiding. She was making a concerted effort to downplay the entire incident.

"Unfortunately, children wander off from their parents more often than we might like," she said, her voice slightly high-pitched and anxious-sounding. "In this case, we are delighted little Shane was discovered alive and well."

"Was the boy's absence related in any way to the body discovered in the mortuary this morning?" a reporter asked.

"Not at all. Purely an unfortunate coincidence."

Margo fumed. "Doesn't that woman know she's putting other lives in jeopardy?" she hissed. "I have half a mind to hold my own press conference. That would show the city fathers—"

"Easy, babe. If we make a fuss now, we'll draw so much attention to the mortuary I won't be able to do the extermination job I have in mind. It's better if we keep calm, handle things quietly and then blow this place.''

Easy for Kane to say. He had somewhere to go. And he hadn't invited her to come along. Not that she expected him to. They hadn't known each other long. The fact that they'd been intimate didn't come with any long-term guarantees. Margo knew that and hated the way she wished things could be different. In spite of everything, she was still a starry-eyed Iowa farm girl who believed in the forever kind of love. Some women never learn....

Before they could escape through the crowd, the mayor spotted them, did a quick dismissal of the reporters and ushered Kane and Margo back inside the mortuary. By now the paramedics had left with the little boy and the three of them had the building to themselves.

''I owe you both an apology,'' the mayor began. ''I'm truly sorry we didn't take your story more seriously.''

Startled by the mayor's about-face, Margo glanced at Kane to check his reaction.

''That and a couple of bucks will get you a cup of coffee almost anywhere in town,'' he said coldly.

''I deserved that,'' the mayor conceded. Her hands trembled slightly as she smoothed her gray hair, and beneath a light covering of makeup she looked pale. ''The fact is, I need your help. The city is right on the

edge financially. In order to keep up city services...
Well, none of that matters now. A child nearly died.''

"Somehow, you weren't all that concerned when it
was a bag lady who'd died,'' Margo said pointedly.
"Penelope, after all, wasn't exactly a registered voter
and that child's parents probably vote in every election.''

"I deserved that, too.'' She smiled wanly. "I don't
suppose you'd believe I once led a League of Women
Voters study of the welfare system and was known as
a flaming liberal.''

Margo didn't respond.

"I'm also a grandmother, Ms. Stafford. My grand-
son is about the same age as Shane, the little boy who
went missing. I couldn't bear the thought if my
Donie...'' Obviously agitated, and motivated by
something other than political ambition, the mayor
glanced from Margo back to Kane. "Do you two
know what it is that is doing these awful things?''

"I have a reasonably good theory,'' he said.

"Do you... Is there any way to eliminate it?''

"Possibly.''

"I'm fully prepared to level the entire building, if
that's what it takes.''

"I doubt that would do the job.''

"Do you have something else in mind?''

"Yes.'' His answer hung in the air along with a
million questions he wasn't prepared to talk about.

The mayor was visibly beginning to sweat, little beads of moisture forming at her hairline. "I don't want to have to go public on this if we can possibly avoid it. I really do have the best interests of the city at heart, but I also don't want anyone else to die. Is there anything I can do...the city can do to assist you?"

Kane's forehead scrolled into a frown. "I need a truck. A big one."

"I'll tell the transportation department to give you whatever you need, whenever you need it."

"This afternoon. As soon as possible. And I also want authority to be in the building without anyone else around. It's likely to be dangerous."

Margo gasped. "You can't do this alone, Kane."

He shot her a silencing look that was fully as irritating as it was frightening.

"You'll have the full cooperation of the city," the mayor assured him. She extended her hand to seal the agreement, but Kane didn't respond.

Neither did Margo.

"About your employment, Ms. Stafford. The city manager may have been a bit hasty in discharging you. If matters work out satisfactorily, I'm sure he may wish to reconsider his decision. I suspect that's also true for you, Officer Rainer."

Her offer could have been an olive branch, or a dual bribe, and at this point Margo didn't much care.

"Just get me what I need to do the job, Your Honor," Kane said.

As the mayor and Kane began to make plans for him to pick up a truck at the city yard, Margo turned and marched out of the mortuary without so much as a by-your-leave. Kane was going to do something courageous. And totally stupid. There was nothing she could do to stop him.

Her chin quivered.

She hated feeling so helpless; she hated loving and not being loved in return. She ought to be packing, she ought to be getting her possessions out of the mortuary, but some perverse instinct drove her toward Kane's house, as if it was a safe haven. In terms of her heart, that certainly wasn't the case.

"Yoo-hoo, Margo, dear." Mrs. Cornelius hurried across the street to meet her. Algernon, tugging on a long leash, traveled twice the distance as his mistress, racing back and forth, his ears flopping, his oversize feet padding along happily.

Margo stifled a groan. She really didn't have the energy to deal with the neighborhood busybody just now.

"I just wanted you to know, dear, how sad I am about Penelope dying. So dreadful." She scooped the dog into arms covered in age spots and gave him a hug. "I wanted you to know how sorry I am for thinking... Well, you understand."

"It seems to be a day for apologies," Margo said.

The older woman's gray eyes grew serious and she rubbed her cheek against the top of Algernon's head. "It appears I've misjudged that young man of yours, just like I made some false assumptions about people who are homeless."

"You mean Kane?" Her young man?

"All these years...well, they say he saved that little child's life. Perhaps he wasn't as bad a boy as I remembered."

"He's as fine a man as I have ever met. Seems to me that's what counts."

"I suppose I'm just a foolish old woman, but I've seen you two together and I thought...since you and he seem to be, you know, living together...and I wasn't too kind when he came back home." A blush blossomed on her wrinkled cheeks. "I'd like to welcome you both to the neighborhood."

Nonplussed, Margo didn't quite know what to say. She wasn't *living* with Kane, exactly, but she was glad Mrs. Cornelius no longer felt such animosity toward him. "Thank you. I'll tell Kane how you feel."

"You do that, dear." She patted Margo lightly on the arm, rather the way she might reassure Algernon that his behavior was acceptable. "And I really think you ought to marry him, dear. Good men are indeed hard to find, you know. Better not to let one of the good ones get away. But I'm so old-fashioned, maybe it simply isn't done that way anymore.''

Now it was Margo's turn to feel the heat of a blush. She might have been thinking about forever-afters, but Kane certainly hadn't expressed any interest.

"Oh, there he comes now," Mrs. Cornelius said. "I'll just run along. I'm hoping if I give Algernon enough exercise, he'll be so tired he won't dig up my roses anymore. He's such a pest, but mercy, how I love him." She smiled, waved at Kane and proceeded down the street with Algernon leading the way, tugging on his leash.

Kane reached Margo's side a moment later.

"I've got the truck all arranged with the city."

Margo headed for the house, aware of an ache that was forming under her breastbone. "You shouldn't be doing this alone."

"I've done things alone all of my life, Margo. It's hard to stop now."

"Mrs. Cornelius has decided you're an asset to the neighborhood. You don't have to prove anything anymore."

He made a humorless sound as he opened the back door. "Too little, too late, I'd say."

The ache in her chest moved up a notch and filled her throat. "You could be hurt."

"Not that Mrs. Cornelius or anyone else would care."

She whirled on him. Right there in the middle of his cozy little kitchen with its cluttered tile counter and aging yellow paint, she raised her fist and was going to smack him one, when she realized the look in his silver-blue eyes was one of fear. Not fear of challenging the monster, but the unholy terror of being alone, a fear he'd lived with his whole life.

Her throat closed so painfully she could only whisper, "Dammit, Kane, I care. And I'm not going to let you do this by yourself."

His big, strong hands framed her face in a tender parenthesis. "I have to."

"No, you don't. I'll go with you in the truck and then we'll—"

"Can't. We're talking heavy-duty security here. The equipment I need is about as classified as it gets. All very hush-hush stuff."

"Can't you tell me anything about this equipment you're going after?"

He hesitated a beat, as though deciding how much she needed to know. "Did you take physics?"

"In high school. It wasn't exactly my best subject."

"Remember when your teacher demonstrated a Jacob's ladder?" When she frowned, he continued. "In its simplest form, it's an electrical device that steps up the wall voltage. The current arcs between two parallel wires, traveling up to the top like it was climbing a ladder.''

"I vaguely remember something like that."

"Without getting too specific or technical, this thing that I'm going after operates on the same general principle as a Jacob's ladder, but it's much more powerful. It's called a Mobil Perimeter Force Field. Once it's set up, nothing—not a tank or even a mosquito—can get through it. And anything that makes the attempt has its atoms rearranged."

Picturing the effects on an enemy soldier, she shivered. "That sounds dangerous."

"Only for the bad guys."

She didn't necessarily believe a Star-Trekky force field was risk free to the operator, but she doubted Kane would change his plans because of her fears. "When you get back, I'll be here to help you."

One corner of his lips twitched into a half smile. "You're real stubborn, you know that?"

"And you're too bossy."

"I'm beginning to like stubborn."

"Bossy is never going to be on my list of top ten."

"How 'bout this?"

He dipped his head and Margo felt the instant budding of arousal as his lips met hers. So quickly, she mused, it was almost as if her body was completely in tune with Kane's. His needs were hers and she responded accordingly.

If she couldn't convince him that he no longer had to tilt at evil windmills alone, at least here, in his arms, she could show him his days of being an outcast were over. She'd give him all the love she had to give, all the passion she'd never before been allowed to express. If, in the end, her heart was shattered, she'd risk that as surely as he was willing to risk his life destroying the hungry creature that inhabited the bowels of the earth beneath the mortuary.

They barely made it to the couch in the living room. Her panty hose and underwear fell by the wayside, and his jeans and boots dropped away. But for the rest, being naked was less important than joining and feeling the hard velvety length of him inside her. Thrusting. To each of his powerful strokes, she answered with the unspoken message that he need no longer feel isolated. In return, he healed her old wounds of inadequacy. She reveled in the newfound power and joy of being a woman.

When he collapsed on her, drained, and she felt thoroughly sated, Margo smiled a sanguine grin. Damn, she was good! And so was Kane.

Kane adjusted his position so he could cradle Margo in his arms more comfortably. There wasn't much room here on the couch. But he didn't want to let go of her. Not just yet.

He'd returned to Torrance two years ago to find some answers. What he had found instead was Margo. Amazingly, she'd made those same answers unimportant. Simply by believing in him, she had lifted the weight of guilt from his shoulders. Even the burden of being the son of a murderer seemed lighter now.

She didn't seem to care.

He might never know the full truth of what happened to Alby. With the cleansing sweep of Margo's absolution, it didn't matter so much anymore. Kane felt he could at last put the past behind him and get on with his life.

Except for the small detail of killing the lingering spirit of his brother. A matter of family pride, he thought grimly, hoping his theory about how to destroy the green mist was right.

He kissed the crown of Margo's head. "Gotta go, babe."

"I wish you wouldn't."

"I want to get to Camp Pendleton and back before it gets dark. It'll take a while to set things up."

"I'll help you."

"I'll let you carry the heavy stuff."

She punched him. Not hard, of course, but he grunted as if she'd hurt him. "I'm sorry. I didn't mean—"

"Shh. I'll live." Sliding out from under her, Kane gave her another quick kiss. "The sooner I get going, the faster we'll have this all behind us."

And then what? he wondered briefly before his concentration shifted into a killing mode. Marines learned to do that if they were going to survive. Kane fully intended to live to tell the tale.

Sunset streaked the tropical clouds blood red. As the air cooled, the afternoon sea breeze dropped to dead calm, stranding a blowing piece of paper in the middle of the street. The leaves on the willow tree in the adjacent yard hung listlessly in the darkening twilight. Deepening shadows crept ominously upward on the walls of the mortuary in the same way fear stole into Margo's awareness.

Kane should have been back by now.

She sat on his front-porch steps, her arms wrapped around her knees, like an adolescent waiting for her boyfriend to show up. Anxious he wouldn't appear at all and equally unsure of what might happen if he did.

Lord, she wished Kane hadn't mentioned anything about her having babies again. It made her feel too achy, too needy, her arms too empty. Her sons were almost too big to hug, much less to hold in her arms or cuddle on her lap. She'd squandered her youth on a man who had only wanted her as an ornament for his high-powered friends to see.

Her cheeks flushed at the very idea of having Kane's children. In spite of herself, she ached to see those silver-blue eyes of his gazing up at her from a crib, or that devastating smile he was so parsimonious about sharing. He ought to laugh more, too, she mused. It was a wondrous sound, coming from so deep in his broad chest.

With a shake of her head, she set aside her wayward thoughts.

She should check the doors at the mortuary to be sure they were locked. She didn't want anyone else to innocently wander inside. As Penelope had. And the little boy.

But she didn't want to go there by herself. The thought terrified her.

If Kane got back too late, tomorrow would be soon enough for him to use his high-tech electronic device against the mist. If they waited until morning, they could be sure *it* was asleep.

Though it seemed to be quiet now. At least Margo wasn't hearing its taunting voice in her head. Only her own mental machinations.

Restless, she stood and paced across the yard. An azalea bush next to the porch looked dusty and in need of water. She found the hose and turned it on.

Even if she did get her job back, would she ever feel comfortable living in a building that had held such terror for her? Forget she couldn't imagine the pain of looking out the window at Kane's house every day and knowing she'd never see him again.

Still, if the creature could be killed and the mortuary made safe, what choice did she have? Working there would certainly be better than living in her car.

Behind her she heard a soft "woof" and turned to see Algernon standing in her yard, tail wagging, and Mrs. Cornelius nowhere in sight.

"You've escaped again, haven't you, boy?" At the cost of another rosebush, Margo suspected, if his muddy paws were any indication.

She squatted to Algernon's level. His whole body quivered with happiness. Just as she reached to snare him by the collar, he whipped away and circled her in delighted frenzy.

"Come on, Algernon. Let's get you back home where you belong."

She took a step toward him, but he darted off in another direction. "Here, boy! Come!"

Obviously Algernon hadn't taken a single doggy-discipline class yet.

Shaking her head, Margo trudged after him as he led her across the street. If he'd just hold still a minute, she could catch up with him, but every time she got within reach, he darted merrily away.

"I'm getting tired of your games," Margo grumbled. Figuring there was no way she could win this particular contest, she turned back, then halted in her tracks.

Algernon was heading directly toward the mortuary.

"No!" She whirled and ran after the dog but that only filled him with enthusiasm for the chase.

He dodged into the patio area, that sheltered alcove where Margo suspected Penelope had lingered, listening to her voices.

Breathless, she rounded the corner, confident she had Algernon trapped in the relatively small enclosure.

Wrong!

He was gone and the side door to the mortuary stood wide open.

"Algernon!" Oh, God, she couldn't go inside there after him. Not alone. Not in the darkening shadows. Not when the green mist might be wakening from its afternoon nap.

She halted by the door. Listening.

Her pulse pounded in her ears with a deafening roar.

The mortuary remained silent. Empty save for the tapping of Algernon's toenails on the plywood floor. Heading toward the basement door.

Margo felt sick to her stomach. She couldn't bear the thought of Mrs. Cornelius losing another dog. Not the same way she had lost Poopsie. Nor could Margo tolerate the possibility that this profane place with its evil mist would commit another atrocity on some innocent victim. Enough lives had been lost.

She edged into the room. Her ragged breathing clashed with the silence like cymbals in an empty concert hall.

"Here, Algernon," she whispered as softly as she could, desperately afraid of waking the mist. "Come here, baby."

On tiptoe, foolishly so, she hurried across the room and switched on the overhead lights. Muted color from dusty antique chandeliers bathed the empty chapel room.

"Dammit, Algernon!" she called. "Come back here!"

If Kane were here, he'd tell her the dog wasn't worth risking her life for—much less her assorted bodily fluids. And he'd probably be right.

But the mist was still asleep.

She could tell by the eerie silence in the building, the hollow vastness that went well beyond the walls, deep into the earth.

She swallowed hard when she discovered the basement door standing open. Why hadn't she, or Kane, or *someone* thought to close it this morning?

Downstairs she could hear Algernon sniffing around, oblivious to the danger. If she didn't get him out of there quickly, he'd wake the mist.

Margo pulled her trembling lower lip between her teeth. God, she was scared. But Algernon . . .

As long as the mist stayed asleep, they'd both be all right.

A stair creaked as it accepted her weight. Margo cringed.

Behind her, the open basement door admitted a rectangular spill of light from upstairs, just enough illumination so she could find her way but not enough brightness to drive away the shadows from the farthest corners of the room.

Algernon gave another happy "woof" and appeared in the middle of the room, his tail still wagging. He'd certainly led her on a merry chase—from his point of view.

She all but herded him into a corner where he wouldn't be able to get away.

With a lunge, she caught him in her arms, breathed a sigh of relief and turned.

Ally-ally-oxen-free. I'm glad you came to play with me.

Be nice to the lady, Albert.

I don't have to.

Bad things happen to little boys who aren't nice.

Margo stared mesmerized as the green mist licked toward her with grasping tentacles, the undulating mass combining with the putrid smell of decay in a hypnotic alliance. A silken thread whipped out to circle her ankles with its stinging cord. She gasped, but she didn't seem able to move as another thread built on the first and the beginnings of a cocoon formed.

She heard a chilling scream and knew it was her own.

CHAPTER THIRTEEN

Kane tried to tamp down his frustration.

It had been bad enough that Colonel Hickman had delayed him, determined to coax Kane back onto active duty with the Marine Corps. And an overly zealous guard had made a federal case of a civilian truck picking up classified equipment, even though Kane was in military dungarees and had plenty of ID.

Then he'd had to contend with a horrendous traffic jam on the San Diego Freeway. Even now, the traffic lights conspired against him, making his progress on the surface streets no faster than a snail's pace.

It was already too late to set up the Perimeter Force Field tonight. Not that he couldn't do it in the dark. He simply wanted the luxury of being able to work while the mist would most likely be sleeping.

But every minute added to his journey intensified his general feeling of unease. Some sixth sense was gnawing away at the edges of his consciousness. It was like knowing there was a sniper nearby, or a booby trap that was about to be triggered, and not being able to identify the illusive source of the threat.

He'd felt this gut-tightening tension before. In the Gulf War. And, as a kid, when he'd gone in search of Alby. The same whisper of fear that had stroked him then did so again, at first like the wind sighing through taut wires. Then louder and more insistent, so terrifying he remembered wanting to run. Every instinct cried out for him to escape!

Resisting the impulse that had driven him years ago, Kane accelerated the panel truck past a slow-moving Datsun, then turned left off of Torrance Boulevard onto the angled street that cut in front of the mortuary.

The lights were on in the building, spilling out of decorative windows downstairs and visible as a faint glow on the second floor. Kane's stomach muscles involuntarily contracted again. That could only mean trouble.

He whipped the vehicle to the left side of the empty street, and with gears grinding, slammed it into reverse, backing it up to the main doors. If it hadn't been for the steps and a porch overhang, he would have driven right on inside.

Almost before the truck quit vibrating, he was out of the cab, trying to open the mortuary door.

Locked. Solid oak doors dead-bolted closed. It would take a tank to open them.

He glanced toward his house, nothing but a dark shadow beyond the streetlights, and knew in his gut Margo wasn't there.

She was here. In the mortuary. And if the mist was awake, it would kill her. Kane might already be too late.

Using instincts honed to battle readiness, he sprinted for the side entrance.

She was going to die.

The cloying scent of dead flowers clung to the back of Margo's throat, making her gag. Lethargy dragged at her willpower. At some intellectual level, she knew she should be able to walk away from the venomous strokes of the mist as it tried to cocoon her. But her body refused to respond to the commands of her brain. In an obscene way, the mist was seducing her. Violating her.

Algernon squirmed in her arms. It wasn't fair the dog had to die, too.

Through a mental fog, she tried to gauge the distance to the opposite side of the writhing mist. If she could toss the puppy that far...

Her arms felt leaden, as though all of her strength had been drained from her body. Perhaps if she just slept for a while...

"Margo! Are you down there?"

Slowly, she raised her head. He'd come for her. Kane, her strength, her love. "Kane...Oh, God, it's got me."

"Hold on, babe, I'm coming. Fight it if you can."

Fight. She could do that. She'd fought to free herself from her husband's oppression. She'd fought back from two years of unemployment, losing her beautiful children and living in her car. She'd survived, dammit, and she could survive this, too.

A surge of adrenaline pumped through her veins and the mist seemed to loosen its deadly grip.

You can't go. You promised to play with me.

"Oh, no, I didn't." She gritted her teeth. Like someone who had been paralyzed for years, she painstakingly placed one foot in front of the other, fighting the hypnotic pull of the mist's intrusive force.

The silken green threads around her legs parted with a soft, shredding sound.

You're not very nice.

Leave her alone, Albert.

You're not the boss of me.

Somebody ought to take a stick to your bottom, young man.

Retreating, the long gaseous tentacles curled toward each other like pythons attacking one of their own.

Upstairs there was the clatter and bang of Kane moving heavy equipment.

Margo dashed for the steps.

Caught off guard, one misty arm made a hurried grab for her. Acid burned her ankle and the scent of sizzling flesh rose to her nostrils. She fought down a renewed sense of panic and ignored the pain. Only a few more steps, then she'd be safe.

She stumbled. Algernon tumbled from her arms. Yapping and whining, he scooted upstairs and through the door.

Kane cursed.

She staggered upward another few steps before she felt Kane's strong arms around her, lifting her, carrying her the rest of the way to the vestibule where she clung to him, drawing one sobbing breath after another.

"Penelope . . . she distracted Alby. Oh, God, that's how I got away. If she hadn't made him mad . . ."

"Shh, it's all right now, babe. You're okay."

She gulped down another sob. "We've got to kill it, Kane. It can't be allowed to exist another minute."

"I've got Perimeter Force Field about ready to go. If you can make it on your own, I want you out of here. Back to my place where you'll be safe."

Lifting her head, she matched his determined gaze with one of her own. "I'm staying. What can I do to help?"

He didn't argue for long. Even if she was trembling like the proverbial leaf, she wasn't going to give in this time. Kane no longer had to fight his demons alone.

She hauled heavy electrical cables and watched as he connected them to steel-encased probes that looked to be right out of the future. When everything was hooked up, Kane hesitated at the top of the steps. From below, reflected light cast grotesque green shadows across his face. In the grim set of his features, she could see his determination and all the years of loneliness when he'd struggled against an enemy he couldn't even name.

He looked at her, his eyes bleak with pain. He'd donned bulky fire-resistant clothing and a helmet that made him look as if he'd come from outer space. "It feels like I'm about to kill Alby. Penelope, too."

"No, Kane, you're *releasing* them. In some obscene way, that green mist trapped their spirits here in the mortuary. We need to help them get away."

He eyed her, the lines around his mouth taut as he weighed her words. "When I reach the bottom step, turn on the generator." He lowered the visor on his helmet.

She nodded, her throat filling with a knot of fear as he turned and began his cautious descent to the basement. He carried a telescoping probe in each hand, long antennae that he held in the same way an avenging knight would wield a pair of spears. Head held high, he challenged his old enemy, his nemesis.

When he stepped onto the last riser, she threw the switch that sent power surging into the probes. Electricity arced between the two probes like lightning flashes across a backdrop of black storm clouds. Kane edged farther into the basement.

Almost immediately, the heat became intense, the stench of burning, melting concrete and steel nearly overpowering, along with the ugly scent of decay being consumed in an unquenchable fire. The air filled with ozone and thunder shook the ground. It was like being inside a dark cloud during a raging lightning storm. The power pummeled all of Margo's senses at once with noise and smell and blinding white light.

An all-too-human scream arose from the depths, the shrill piercing sound of flesh and sinew drawn painfully taut.

You're hurting me!

I told you if you were bad you were askin' for trouble.

Grimly, Kane continued to advance on the retreating mist.

Pick on someone your own size!

"Give it up, Alby. It's been twenty-five years. It's time to let go."

Suddenly, the mist exploded, dissipating into a million tiny droplets, each caught momentarily in the air, then the gaseous remains fled en masse through the closing cracks in the floor like an escaping river.

Startling quiet returned to the basement with only the hum of a generator and the reek of death remaining. Molten concrete flowed across the floor in a gray slurry, sealing it forever.

Margo took a deep, shuddering breath. "I think I'm about to lose it." She was so near tears, the back of her eyes stung with them and her throat felt clogged. Her legs were as wobbly as a distance runner who had run out of steam; the dark curtain of a faint threatened.

"Hang on a little bit longer, if you can," Kane urged her. "I've gotta get this equipment back in the truck before some nosy neighbor gets too good a look."

Numb, and feeling unfocused, she helped roll up the cables again. But mostly she simply stood in the vestibule, sensing the benign emptiness in the mortuary and trying not to pass out.

Kane did what he had to do.

And then somehow she was at Kane's house, in his old-fashioned living room, and she felt safer than she had in a long, long time.

"I thought I was going to die." There was amazement in her voice as she discovered she was very much alive.

Kane slid his arms around her and pulled her hard against his chest. "I did, too, babe. I was afraid I couldn't get to you in time. Like with Alby."

She looked up at him. "Did you remember?"

"It was more of a feeling." Unconsciously he tucked a few loose strands of her hair behind her ear, but she knew he was thinking of a time twenty-five years ago. "I think I saw Alby that night he didn't come home, and the mist had him. I don't know if he was dead then or not. But I didn't do anything. I was scared and I ran."

"Kane, you were only fourteen. There wasn't any way you could have fought it."

"Maybe. But I was supposed to take care of my brother. Instead, I wimped out."

"And for twenty-five years you've been trying to make up for what you thought was a terrible mistake. It's all over, Kane. It's really all over. There's nothing you could have done."

Lifting her chin, he placed a soft kiss on her lips. "Thanks."

"You saved my life. I should be the one doing the thanking."

His lips hitched into a smile. "I don't know about you, but I could sure use a shower."

"That *thing*..." She shuddered. "Where it touched me, I felt violated. Dirty. I'm not sure I'll ever be able to wash that feeling away."

"You're the best, most pure person I have ever known, Margo. No matter what the mist did to you, there's no way it could make you dirty. Not where it counts, in your heart. It's just not possible."

She smiled a little weakly. "You're a nice man, Kane Rainer."

He responded with a hug. "We'd save water if we showered together."

Margo's agreement came easily.

With remarkable tenderness, Kane lathered her body and shampooed her hair. His hands moved everywhere on her with ultimate familiarity, as though he knew all of those intimate secrets she'd kept hidden so deeply, even from herself.

And when it was his turn, she explored exciting masculine textures of skin and tendons and sinew, and flesh darkened by swirling hair, caressing and stroking until her breathing became ragged, uneven, and her legs grew weak, her heart pounding with need.

With equal care, he dried her with a big fluffy towel. Wrapping it around her, he settled her on the bathroom counter, the room steamy and redolent with a sexual bouquet, while he applied a soothing ointment to burns inflicted on her legs by the green mist.

He carried her into the bedroom where they continued their journey of discovery. At last, Margo could wait no longer. In spite of how much she wanted to linger on the high plateau of desire, she peaked and burst in a shuddering climax as he entered her. While she continued to pulse around him, she drew him deeper and felt his own draining response.

She drifted a while, content with Kane's weight on her and the sound of his slow breathing brushing softly against her ear. Then with a groan, he shifted, settling next to her, his arm resting protectively across her midsection.

The streetlight cast muted shadows into the room, comfortable shadows that no longer hid monsters lurking in the dark corners of her mind.

Idly, Kane's palm flattened across her belly. "So it looks like you'll still have a job if you want it."

She didn't want to come back to reality yet. Not if it meant she would go on as before—alone. "That's what the mayor said."

"Then you'll open the shelter?"

"I suppose. Maybe I'll keep my résumé circulating, but at the moment I don't think I have any other choice but to do what I was hired to do." Her mother had always told her not to ask questions when she wasn't prepared to hear the answer. Yet she had to know... "Any chance you might stay here in Torrance?"

"No. Too many bad memories."

Her mother had been right. Kane's answer was as painful as if she had taken a bullet full in the chest without a vest to protect her. "I thought that would be the case."

"Have you ever thought of moving to Arizona?"

She went very still. Even her heart seemed to draw to a halt and her breath lodged painfully in her lungs. "Arizona?"

"It seems to me we haven't been real careful when we've made love, and I figured if by any chance you were pregnant..."

"When I was married, I was on the Pill. There hasn't been any need—"

"Then something could have happened?"

She paused, willing herself not to leap to conclusions. "You'd want me to have the baby?"

"Sure. If that's what you wanted, I mean. There's a pretty good university at Flagstaff and I'll have a decent job. You could get your master's degree, like you talked about. And since the area's growing, that probably means there are people who need counseling. You'd be good at that."

"Being an unwed mother wouldn't exactly set a good example for my boys."

"Yeah, well, we could probably fix that."

Trying to contain the rush of joy that nearly swamped her, Margo rose up on her elbow. "Just exactly what are you trying to say?"

"I'm the son of a convicted murderer, I've always been a loner and I suspect I'll revert to being bossy from time to time. I'm not a real good catch, Margo."

"Mrs. Cornelius thinks you are."

He scowled, his eyebrows nearly touching in the middle. "I'm not proposing to her, dammit. I'm trying to propose to you and things like this aren't easy for me. I've never proposed before."

"Never?"

"It feels a little like my commanding officer has just ordered me to storm the enemy beach all by myself."

Giddy with happiness, she brushed a straying lock of dark hair away from Kane's forehead. "Do you love me?"

"Hell, yes, and it scares me to death. When that mist had a hold of you...I knew if I lost you, I'd never get over it."

"Oh, Kane, I love you, too, and I'm just as scared as you are. It's all happened so fast."

"Yeah..." He laughed a rough, sexy sound that could have been from relief. "We've both lived a couple of lifetimes in this last week. Maybe we could live the rest of our lives a bit more quietly?"

"With a nice little house in the mountains, and maybe some trees? A big enough place for my sons to come visit?"

"You could settle for that?"

"Settle? It's more than I've dared dream about."

"I could take your kids fishing."

"I think they'd like that."

He hugged her, fiercely, kissing her hard and long. Margo knew she'd never felt such happiness in her entire life.

They made love again just before dawn and afterward Kane dozed. When he wakened, he found himself alone in the big bed that had once belonged to his folks.

For a moment he panicked.

Had he blacked out and dreamed the whole thing with Margo? God, was she gone? Had he deserted her the way he had his brother?

Rolling out of bed, he headed down the hallway at nearly a dead run.

He found her in the living room, sitting on the floor cross-legged in front of the fireplace. A gas flame licked around a single piece of kindling. Relief dragged the air from his lungs and curiosity pulled him to her side.

"Meditating again?" he asked.

Without shifting her attention from the fire, she said, "Not exactly. More like doing a little housekeeping."

"Isn't the weather still a little warm for a fire?"

"Not this fire. You should have burned it years ago."

Puzzled, he squatted beside her. "Burned what?"

"That slat from the bunk bed. You're not a killer, Kane, and you never could be. I decided the best way to put the past behind us and start over was to begin by getting rid of that worthless chunk of wood."

His chest filled with an emotion so powerful it could only be love. Already the fire had scorched the *ILL* so that it was no longer readable. In a minute the fire would consume the rest of the letters, too, along with the painful reminder Kane had faced every morning and night of his youth.

He levered himself up to a sitting position on the couch and pulled Margo with him. "Now, why didn't I think of doing that?"

"Because you let others lock you in the past, Kane. It's all gone now. Every bit of it."

"And your past, Margo? Is that all behind you?"

"Except for my boys, absolutely. I'm more than ready to focus on the future now. Our future together."

Kane liked the sound of that. Until now, he'd never much cared about what would happen the next day, or week, or even the next year. Now, as he drew Margo into his arms, he looked forward to all the tomorrows they'd have together.

*   *   *   *   *

Welcome To The
Dark Side Of Love...

COMING NEXT MONTH

#63 OLD FLAMES—Sandra Dark

James Shockley had no idea he'd been living above an unholy burial ground, one Dr. Amber Sheridan called the find of a lifetime. But James found nothing earth-shattering about the age-old crypt, while everything Amber did or said struck a chord within him. She seemed eerily familiar, sensually provocative. And as a strange darkness gripped at his soul, James knew his desire for Amber was both destined—and dangerous....

COMING IN TWO MONTHS

#64 GOOD NIGHT, MY LOVE—Jeanne Rose

Adriana Thorne loved everything about the night—the pulsing energy, the dark mystery, the sensuality.... Enigmatic newcomer Valentin Kadar embodied all her midnight fantasies and so much more. But Val's arrival coincided strangely with three grisly murders—all close friends of Adriana's. And when her sister turned up missing, Adriana could only pray that her nocturnal lover wasn't instead a ruthless predator of the night....

It's time you joined...

THE BABY OF THE MONTH CLUB

Silhouette Desire proudly presents *Husband:
Optional,* book four of RITA Award-winning
author Marie Ferrarella's miniseries,
THE BABY OF THE MONTH CLUB, coming
your way in March 1996.

She wasn't fooling him. Jackson Cain knew the
baby Mallory Flannigan had
borne was his...no matter that
she *claimed* a conveniently
absentee lover was Joshua's
true dad. And though Jackson
had left her once to "find" his true
feelings, nothing was going to
keep him away from this
ready-made family now....

Do You Take This Child? We
certainly hope you do, because
in April 1996 Silhouette Romance
will feature this final book in
Marie Ferrarella's wonderful
miniseries, THE BABY OF THE MONTH CLUB, found
only in— 🌹 *Silhouette*®
™

Bestselling author

RACHEL LEE

takes her Conard County series to new heights with

A CONARD COUNTY Reckoning

This March, Rachel Lee brings readers a brand-new, longer-length, out-of-series title featuring the characters from her successful Conard County miniseries.

Janet Tate and Abel Pierce have both been betrayed and carry deep, bitter memories. Brought together by great passion, they must learn to trust again.

"Conard County is a wonderful place to visit! Rachel Lee has crafted warm, enchanting stories. These are wonderful books to curl up with and read. I highly recommend them."
—*New York Times* bestselling author
Heather Graham Pozzessere

Available in March, wherever Silhouette books are sold.

Alicia Scott's

THE GUINESS GANG

Elizabeth, Mitch, Cagney, Garret and Jake:

Four brothers and a sister—though miles separated them, they would always be a family.

Don't miss a single, suspenseful—sexy—tale in Alicia Scott's family-based series, which features four rugged, untamable brothers and their spitfire sister:

THE QUIET ONE...IM #701, March 1996

THE ONE WORTH WAITING FOR...IM #713, May 1996

THE ONE WHO ALMOST GOT AWAY...IM #723, July 1996

Order the first two books in the series: AT THE MIDNIGHT HOUR, IM#658 and HIDING JESSICA, IM#668. Send your name, address, zip or postal code, along with a cheque or money order (please do not send cash) for $3.75 for each book ordered ($4.25 in Canada) plus 75¢ postage and handling ($1.00 in Canada) payable to Silhouette Books, to:

In the U.S.	In Canada
Silhouette Books	Silhouette Books
3010 Walden Ave.	P. O. Box 636
P. O. Box 9077	Fort Erie, Ontario
Buffalo, NY 14269-9077	L2A 5X3

Please specify book title(s) with your order.
Canadian residents add applicable federal and provincial taxes.

"The Guiness Gang," found only in—

the exciting series by
NEW YORK TIMES BESTSELLING AUTHOR

Nora Roberts

The MacKade Brothers are back—looking for trouble,
and always finding it. Coming this March,
Silhouette Intimate Moments presents

THE HEART OF DEVIN MACKADE
(Intimate Moments #697)

If you liked THE RETURN OF RAFE MACKADE (Silhouette
Intimate Moments #631) and THE PRIDE OF JARED MACK-
ADE (Silhouette Special Edition #1000), you'll love Devin's
story! Then be on the lookout for the final book in the series,
THE FALL OF SHANE MACKADE (Silhouette Special Edition
#1022), coming in April from Silhouette Special Edition.

 These sexy, trouble-loving
men heading out to you in
alternating books from
Silhouette Intimate Moments and
Silhouette Special Edition. Watch out for them!

Yo amo novelas con corazón!

Starting this March, Harlequin opens up to a whole new world of readers with two new romance lines in SPANISH!

Harlequin Deseo
- passionate, sensual and exciting stories

Harlequin Bianca
- romances that are fun, fresh and very contemporary

With four titles a month, each line will offer the same wonderfully romantic stories that you've come to love—now available in Spanish.

Look for them at selected retail outlets.

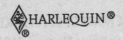

**This March
come back to
where it all began with**

DESTINATION: CONARD COUNTY

Return to Conard County—where passions
match the wild terrain under blue Wyoming skies.

Back by popular demand, the first two Conard
County stories by Rachel Lee—all in one special
collection!

**EXILE'S END
CHEROKEE THUNDER**

And don't forget to look for *A Conard County
Reckoning*, the newest addition to the Conard
County family. Available this March wherever
books are sold.

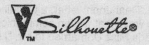

SREQ396

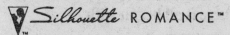